THE PAWPRINTS COLLECTION

DARA GIRARD

CONTENTS

Collections

Domestic Disturbance (written as Dara Benton)

The Lady Next Door and Other Stories

Holiday Hearts

School Days: Five Story Collection

Lost and Found

Five Holiday Tales

10 Holiday Stories

When the Snow Falls

Henson Series

Table for Two

Gaining Interest

Careless Rapture

Dangerous Curves

Familiar Stranger

Clifton Sisters

The Sapphire Pendant

The Amber Stone

The Emerald Ring

Novels

Honest Betrayal

The Daughters of Winston Barnett

Remember My Name

Illusive Flame

Winterwood Lane

Piece of Cake

This Changes Everything

PAWPRINTS IN THE SNOW

PAWPRINTS IN THE SNOW

HE WASN'T A CAT PERSON. He didn't like cats. He didn't think they were cute or sweet or interesting. He didn't like to think of them at all. But when Paul Gibbons opened his front door one sunny December afternoon and saw a skinny cat—one of those fussy, squashed faced breeds with black and white fur—looking on the verge of death, he couldn't turn away. As much as he wanted to. And he tried. He made a half-hearted attempt to scare it away, but the cat just blinked.

He searched his sparse kitchen—he usually ordered in and hadn't gone grocery shopping in the small Maryland town where he'd settled the past several years—until he found some tuna. He checked the can to see the "sell-by" date to make sure the can wasn't too old. He couldn't remember the last time he'd eaten anything out of a can and didn't want to feed the cat something that would make it sick. Not that he thought the cat would live very much longer, but he didn't want to be the cause of its early demise.

Once he was certain the tuna was still edible, he put it in a small cracked saucer and left it out for the cat to eat. But the cat wouldn't touch it. The three times he would check outside his window to see if the animal was still there, he saw the saucer bowl still untouched. He softly swore then stepped outside to confront the cat. "Look, you eat or you die," he said.

The cat just looked up at him, its expression more miserable than before.

This is why he didn't like cats. They were high maintenance and picky.

"I can't help you," he said and started to close the door, the cat's green eyes watching him with an intensity that made his skin crawl. Yes, this was the other reason he didn't like cats. They were complicated and knew too much about him.

But he wasn't going to be swayed. He wouldn't leave it to die, but he wouldn't get too close either. He'd get this cat healthy and then out of his life, just as he had everything else that caused him trouble. And cats had always been the source of his greatest trouble, but he gently lifted the cat, feeling it was more bones then flesh, and went inside.

HE FOUND out from the vet, a woman with big teeth and too much mascara, that the cat was a female. Paul pretended not to know, even though he already did. He knew a lot more than he wanted to about his squashed faced intruder. He had always known too much about things, but he had learned to feign ignorance. He pretended not to know that the cat had bad teeth and probably had once been loved and then discarded—likely by an uncaring relative who had left it on the street to die.

At first he even pretended not to know that her name was Phillipa. She'd been named by her owner, a woman who'd had her for ten years before she got sick.

Phillipa wanted to tell him more, but he wasn't interested. The story of an elderly owner falling on hard times and a beloved pet suffering the consequences was nothing new. And he didn't want to care. Although Phillipa tried to slip him information, he made sure to keep his mind blank.

He just listened to the diagnosis from the vet and took notes on what he needed to do to make sure Phillipa got well. To their disappointment—more his than the vet's—Phillipa didn't have a chip so they couldn't find out who her true owner was. She also didn't have a collar.

She loved wearing collars; she managed to sneak into his thoughts like a careful whisper, on their drive home. She missed her old one. A sparkly number with her name engraved. Could she get another one?

No.

After getting her teeth fixed, she ate with the ferocity of a lion. She didn't like tuna or salmon. Chicken was fine, but she preferred fresh mice if possible.

No. It wasn't possible.

He didn't want her giving him orders. Once she was healthy again she was leaving. He'd kept her longer than he should have anyway.

A WEEK later Paul sat in his living room staring at the tiny Christmas tree he'd decorated for no reason at all. He knew there'd be no one else to see it but him. And he wasn't really a holiday person, but since Phillipa's arrival he'd wanted to do something so he wouldn't think about her. Think about what having her there meant to him, said about him.

She kept her distance. He was glad for that. Cats were smart. They knew boundaries. Most times, except when they were trying to reveal who he really was. What he really was.

Phillipa jumped up on the table where the tree sat and sniffed it, her nose touching a purple plastic ornament and causing it to bounce off the table and fall to the ground. She jumped down and batted it between her paws.

Paul shook his head. His little tree looking more pathetic without the ornament, which had helped hide how thin its branches were. *You're supposed to say sorry.*

Why? This is fun. She batted the ornament again then stopped and looked at him. *Will I get something for Christmas?*

No.

She didn't pout, which was good. She'd gotten a place to stay and food. Wasn't that gift enough? Why did people always want more?

Not that he considered her a person. He knew she wasn't, but like every living creature she seemed to stretch and crave and grasp for more.

But he'd hidden away because he had nothing more to give.

Phillipa sat and let her tail sway slowly to the right. *She's still there.*

Paul shifted his gaze to the unlit fireplace. He saw one lonely card from his parents sitting on the black mantelpiece. He didn't know how they found him, but they always seemed to. And every year he put up their card, knowing its cherry colors couldn't hide how alone he was.

Phillipa's tail swayed again, to the left, this time with more force. *She's still there.*

He didn't care. He didn't want to care. Phillipa talked a lot about her former girl who she called Annie. He didn't trust that that was her true name (cats liked to live by their own rules) or even that she was a young girl, (cats didn't care much about age as long as their girls or boys did as told, they didn't feel that being specific was necessary when it came to humans). She was more polite than most who referred to humans as pets. But he still didn't believe the name Phillipa had given Annie was her real one. For all he knew, Phillipa could have named her 'girl' after her favorite brand of chicken hearts.

What he did know, and could trust, was that Phillipa adored—no adored was too strong, cats didn't think like that—highly esteemed her girl. She liked to tell him what Annie liked to wear.

Did that really matter? He once asked her, bored by her description.

Yes, she informed him then continued to talk.

She also talked about how Annie liked to hum old

show tunes. How her book club was always hosted at her house and all the ladies and one guy would coo over Phillipa and how cute she was.

Do you think I'm cute?

No.

But more and more Phillipa talked about Annie's last days. He didn't want to care, but each day he grew more curious. Curious about a woman he imagined to be kind, in her late fifties, and who smelled like nutmeg and Shea butter.

WHAT HAPPENED?

He didn't mean to ask, but his curiosity had gotten the best of him. He stood over Phillipa as she ate a beef and carrot mix.

Phillipa flicked her tail then continued to eat.

Paul sat down beside her and folded his arms. *Don't play games. If you don't tell me now I'll never ask again.*

I'm eating.

He started to stand.

It hurts.

He sat back down and fell silent. He looked at the crooked little tree then heard purring and looked down to see that he'd been stroking her. When had he started doing that and why hadn't he noticed her come up next to him?

He folded his arms.

Phillipa looked up at him. *You know what happened.*

Not the details.

Phillipa continued to stare. *Please.*

He folded his arms tighter. *I can't help you. Haven't I helped you enough?*

She's still there.

Paul rose to his feet and turned on the television sorry he'd asked.

HE DIDN'T SLEEP that night. He closed his door so that Phillipa wouldn't watch him. She'd gotten into the strange habit of watching him go to sleep, her penetrating green cat eyes seeming to glow in the darkness; her body tense, waiting as if she anticipated something.

But it wouldn't work. He was done. Nothing would happen.

He got into bed and stared up at the ceiling and in his mind's eye he saw Annie's brown hand stroking Phillipa, he saw a cane resting against the couch within easy reach. Then he saw Annie's face through Phillipa's eyes and saw she wasn't as old as he'd thought. Pretty. Not that it mattered.

She would walk with a limp for a long time since breaking her leg. *But it wasn't an accident* another voice told him.

He closed his eyes and plugged his ears, although he knew the motion was futile. He still saw the event: The distracted driver barreling towards Annie's car. She was lucky to have survived. But she needed someone to come and help her.

Someone now kept her drugged and had tossed her cat out to die.

She's still there.

Phillipa's voice had become more insistent now-- stronger. She was stronger. He'd even opened the front door to let her out to see if she'd go and disappear, but she always came back.

*T*HERE'S *nothing I can do.*

Paul sat at his kitchen table eating a breakfast burrito he'd heated in the microwave. He wasn't really hungry, but ate anyway. Trying not to be hypnotized by the slow sway of Phillipa's tail as she stared up at him. She didn't speak. Her tail said enough.

No more. It won't help.

Her tail stopped swaying. *It will. You can help.*

I show up on the doorstep and do what? Say I have her cat and I think she's in danger? Do you know what happened last time?

Phillipa licked her paw then cleaned herself. This was why he hated cats. He hated their nonchalance; that total self regard. Here he was sharing his fears and she was grooming herself as if she were in the presence of a manservant. But of course she didn't know what had happened last time. Or maybe she could guess, but didn't care.

She cared about Annie, she cared about herself. She didn't care about him. Few people did. He wouldn't risk his life again.

You can help.

He took a deep breath. He thought about Annie's cane, he thought about how sickly Phillipa had been only a few weeks ago.

I'll just go by the house.

Phillipa paused briefly then continued to groom.

IT WAS COLD. Colder than cold. Paul stood outside a blue and white boxy house, its two windows lit and one car in the carport.

Knock on the door.

Phillipa's command flew over the miles that separated them, her thoughts easily blending with his, as she lazed safe and warm on his brown sofa. *I only said I'd check.*

You have to go inside.

Paul looked at one of the windows and saw the shades had been drawn. They'd lock him away this time.

You can lie. Phillipa told him. *She's home alone. Get her out.*

He found the spare key where Phillipa had told him to look and went inside. A hushed quiet greeted him as he closed the door, the dark scent of dominance lingering in the air. He saw shoes by the door. Tiny petite shoes, they didn't belong to Phillipa's owner.

I don't have an owner! came Phillipa's sharp retort.

Paul softly swore, he had to guard his thoughts more carefully. *Your girl, then.* He corrected.

He studied the shoes again. They weren't Annie's but the woman who was looking after her.

Don't trust her. Phillipa warned.

I won't.

Get out fast.

He followed Phillipa's directions and went directly to Annie's room. He imagined she would open her eyes and scream and call the police. Just like the last time he tried to help someone. The person eventually dropped charges, but it had been an ordeal. He'd briefly revealed himself—who he was, *what* he was—and that had helped only briefly before the campaign against his type began again. Freak. Feline f**ker. There were many myths about how his people came to have such a genetic and psychic tie with cats. There were lots of origin stories, but few knew the truth, just the outcome: A person born with the ability to communicate with cats and see life on a fourth dimensional realm. And there was more—the stuff of nightmares.

He'd left town. He made people nervous. He didn't blame them. He knew too much. He always knew too much. But he'd never used his knowledge to hurt anyone.

He softly knocked on the door.

Just go in.

Paul gritted his teeth. *No.*

She's still there.

I know that.

Then go in and get her.

He walked into the room, ready to hear a scream, ready to duck when she threw something at him.

She did neither. Annie sat up in her bed with pillows surrounding her and stared at him wide eyed.

Phillipa sent me.

I know.

He paused. No screaming. No panic. She sounded sensible. She knew? Did that mean... He didn't have time to question. *We have to hurry.*

She grabbed her cane and got out of bed fully clothed, as if she'd been prepared. As if she'd been waiting for him. He couldn't think about that now either. He had to get her out. He swept her up in his arms when they reached the top of the stairs. He needed to be fast and as much as she tried, she was slowing them down.

They made it down the stairs. He paused when bright car lights lit up the dark room as a car drove up. He felt Annie stiffen.

She bit her lip. *Where's your car?*

It's a block over. She won't see it.

Good.

Maybe you should come back another time.

No we're leaving now.

It was only when he made it to the back door that he realized they hadn't spoken in words. It had seemed so natural, he hadn't noticed. His heart began to pound. He'd never met another one like him.

He wasn't alone. He wasn't crazy. He'd made the right choice to come and get her.

But they still weren't safe. Unless...

"We don't have to run," he said, turning. This was Annie's house and she wouldn't be a prisoner or run away.

"Yes, we do," she said. Her voice made him pause it was low and deep—not quite a purr, not quite a whisper —stirring the hairs on his arms. "She..."

He took a deep breath, gaining courage. "Can't defeat us," he said, liking the feel of the final word in his mouth, his heart again picking up speed. Us. He'd never been an 'us' before. Even his parents hadn't been like him. He'd always been different.

"She's strong."

"Is she like us?" he asked walking to the front door, ready to do battle.

"No, but wait..."

It was too late. The moment he faced the second woman, the owner of the tiny shoes, he realized he should have listened to Annie. He'd become too bold, too cocky. He should have assessed the situation better.

He'd sensed the quiet dominance when he'd entered the house, now he'd met its source. She was another power. The reason Annie hadn't been able to leave, the reason Phillipa had been so weak and had taken days to recover. The dominate energy swirled strong in the petite form. He stumbled back at first, afraid he'd drop Annie and injure her more.

The woman smiled. A feline smile. Paul half expected her to lick her lips in anticipation of a fine meal.

She's mine, the woman said with her dark brown eyes as two cats emerged from the shadows.

Don't run. It was a command from Phillipa, not Annie.

He froze. Not because she told him to, but because he couldn't move. He felt paralyzed.

No he *was* paralyzed by her. She harnessed and manipulated his energy causing his bones to feel like lead, the weight of her power holding him hostage.

The power his parents had tried to hide him from when they'd sent him away, the power that the others thought he had, but didn't. It was creatures like her that made the rest of them pariahs. All he could do was save, he couldn't destroy. That was his weakness.

Paul fought to keep a scream from escaping him, his skin feeling as if it was being ripped and torn by claws, and tiny teeth gnawing at his flesh with an insatiable hunger. He fought not to surrender to the powerful dominance of a true predator.

And a predator always needed prey, it couldn't survive without it. And he'd been prey all his life. Hidden and hunted.

But he wouldn't hide tonight. He felt Annie's body tremble and felt rage instead of fear and that rage broke through the paralysis, tore through the fear. He would fight because he didn't fear dying. He would fight because he had to save Annie and Phillipa. Phillipa needed him too.

And he felt the energy in the room shift. The two cats at the woman's side hesitated and just that moment of hesitation gave him the fuel he needed. With lightening speed he swung Annie to his back then pounced. He killed the woman with a swipe of his hand, her neck snapping like a toothpick. Hot blood rushed through his veins as he watched her body go limp.

"Come," Annie said in an urgent whisper, her arms

wrapped around his neck. "She won't stay that way for long."

He knew that but he still waited. He waited and just as suspected her form changed and soon she was the same shape and size as her two companions her glowing eyes glared up at him and she hissed, flashing her teeth. He wondered how many lives she'd given up to bargain her way into human form.

"Can we go now?" Annie asked.

Paul turned to her confused. "But you're safe now. You can..." He let his words fall away when she shook her head.

"I can't stay here not tonight, please. I just want to see Phillipa."

He hesitated. He didn't know why. The threat was gone, but he felt a different kind of unease. He'd never had anyone stay at his place before. He hadn't thought his plan through...

"I can stay at a hotel," Annie said quickly, sensing his hesitation.

"No, it's okay," he said, trying to convince himself that it was. That *he* was. But his heart continued to race with a new fear he couldn't place.

Do I frighten you? she asked on the drive to his home. The softly falling snow hitting his windscreen, the night was dark, but he didn't have trouble seeing.

Was that it? Was he frightened of her? He'd just proven how powerful he was, why was he still scared?

No he said.

Phillipa greeted them at the door and he watched the reunion with a detached eye. He saw Phillipa curl around Annie's leg. Phillipa purred at Annie's touch; Annie beamed down at her with joy. And as he watched the pair, he realized his fear had a name—loss.

He would lose Phillipa and he would miss her. He was being tossed aside, again. He'd grown attached when he shouldn't have. He hadn't wanted to, but he'd failed. Phillipa had made him want to belong and not be alone anymore. He turned to head to his bedroom. Phillipa would show Annie around the house.

Where are you going? Phillipa asked.

Come join us. Annie added.

He paused. Were they just being polite? He faced them. He gripped his hands into fists, wanting to be with the two so much it embarrassed him. "You two have a lot to catch up on."

"No we don't," Annie said with a laugh as she took a seat on his couch.

Her laugh awoke something in him as he realized why she was amused. She and Phillipa had been in contact the whole time, just as he had been able to communicate with Phillipa from miles away, time and distance hadn't separated them. Nothing truly separated them and they were welcoming him into the fold. No, they were telling him he was already there. They'd found each other. His heart felt buoyant.

I'll make a fire.

Moments later they all sat in front of the fireplace, the sound of crackling flames mingling with the faint scent of burning wood filling the room.

"Is your name really Annie?"

"No," she said with a laugh. "It's Phillipa. She told me your name was Rocky."

Paul glared down at the sneaky cat that pretended to be asleep. Cats just couldn't be trusted.

"She's getting salmon tomorrow."

Phillipa—Annie—lifted her head and licked Paul's hand, her rough tongue teasing his skin, by way of apology.

He sighed, feeling his heart melt for both of them.

The next day a one-eyed cat appeared on his front door, but he didn't hesitate letting him into the house or hearing his story. Paul knew what he needed to do and he wouldn't run from who or what he was anymore, but the cat's problem would have to wait until the New Year.

PAWPRINTS IN THE HEART

PAWPRINTS IN THE HEART

HE STILL WASN'T a cat person. Not really. Sure, only two months ago a squashed faced black and white intruder named Annie had crashed into his life and introduced him to his new—wonderful, amazing, kind, beautiful—girlfriend, Phillipa, but that didn't mean he liked cats.

He didn't hate them. They just proved a nuisance. Especially Annie who didn't like to keep her opinions to herself. *What are you getting her for Valentines' Day,* she'd asked him yesterday. *Not flowers.*

Paul was more annoyed by the fact that he didn't know his response, than by the question. He'd lived most of his life in hiding. Away from everyone else, even his parents who he knew loved him, but he wanted to keep them safe. He never thought he'd meet another one like himself until Phillipa entered his life. Within one week he knew that he'd met his heartmate, but he didn't let himself hope that she would return his feelings. It was a shy smile and a light kiss on New Year's Eve that told him she did. And now a day of expressing ones love was coming and he didn't know what to get her.

Why not flowers? He asked Annie as he cleaned up the dishes from breakfast.

Annie sat by his feet. If he moved too fast he could accidentally step on her paw or tail, but that prospect never seemed to bother her. *Just because,* she said.

That's not an answer.

What will you get me?

I'm not getting you anything.

Crickets would be nice.

I'm not getting you anything.

Fine...fine...chicken hearts.

You're not listening.

He left the house for peace. A light snowstorm had swept through the small Maryland town, leaving patches of white among the brown tree trunks, grey streets, and green grass.

It didn't take him long to realize he was being followed.

He pretended not to notice.

He knew he should have driven to the convenience store, but he wanted the walk. The weather was finally hinting at spring after a brutal winter and he'd been seduced by the clear blue sky and sound of birds. And he wanted to get Phillipa something special. Not at the last minute like most guys do.

Paul didn't look over his shoulder. Perhaps he was being paranoid. There was nothing wrong. He was always careful with how he walked—his natural instinct was to stalk and pause, but his parents had scolded and trained him out of that—so he didn't draw attention to himself.

Minutes later he entered the convenience store, making sure to keep his senses lowered—the lights were a little too bright and he didn't want to pay too much attention to the young man standing in front of the cash register. He had a bad cough and the sweet scent of a diabetic who hadn't kept his sugar level under control. Paul half wanted to tell him to stay away from the six- pack Miller Lite he'd just bought, but he'd learned it was best to keep his opinions to himself.

Safer that way. Always safer to stay away from others.

Except for Phillipa. Phillipa he could trust. The tension within him eased when he thought of her. Because of her he wasn't alone anymore.

Paul walked over to the 'seasonal' aisle that had been cleared of all the December and January holidays items, although there was a three foot high red and green display offering holiday items at eighty-percent off. He walked into the aisle and searched the shelves a little horrified by the screaming, various shades of red that tainted everything from teddy bears to chocolate bars, balloons, candles, balls and even lighters.

He rubbed his chin. What would make her happy? What would be special enough to make her smile? He paused when he saw a heart shaped box of chocolates and a stuffed bear. That would be nice. He happily got his purchases and headed back home.

And realized he was still being followed.

By a long haired grey cat.

He inwardly groaned. Cats were his biggest annoyance because they knew his secret and tended not to leave him alone.

He glanced up at a titmouse perched on a bare branch. Maybe if the cat followed his gaze it would be distracted and focus on the titmouse instead of him. Or maybe, if he focused really hard, he could pretend he wasn't being followed. That the cat wasn't there. That it didn't want to talk to him.

That it didn't...he felt the cat's gaze on the back of his neck.

No, no don't look at it. That's what it wants you to do.

He rubbed the back of his neck and surrendered. He looked back. The cat was still there. Keeping a good distance. It was a few feet away. Enough to let its presence be known, but a good polite distance.

A considerate cat. What an anomaly.

Paul stopped walking. He felt the cat stop too.

He slowly turned.

He half hoped the cat would walk past him. Perhaps what he sensed was all in his mind. Perhaps he'd gotten paranoid, perhaps...

The cat looked at him and sat, meeting his gaze.

Damn.

He turned and picked up his pace. *Leave me alone. I can't help you.*

Yes, you can.

No, I can't. I won't.

Please.

Polite. So damn polite.

It was dangerous to listen. It was dangerous to get involved. He'd learned that even though it had changed his life for the better. But he liked his new routine. He had a place to stay, a woman he loved and who loved him. He wasn't lonely anymore. He was going to give her a gift for Valentines' Day and...

Please.

Paul stopped walking and looked around to make sure they weren't being watched. A black man walking beside a cat usually drew attention and that could be dangerous for both of them. It wasn't a friendly world for people like him. People who had a genetic and psychic connection with cats.

He'd come as a surprise to his parents, who weren't like him, and they did their best to keep him safe and teach him how not to be noticed. It hadn't been easy. He'd moved from city to city, state to state and finally found a place where he'd been able to live, for the last several years, under the radar. He hoped to keep it that way.

But he needed to do something. He bent down and tapped his shoulder.

The cat needed no other invitation, it jumped on his shoulder.

Paul grunted as he straightened. *You're heavier than you look.*

I'm carrying kittens.

He wasn't surprised. She smelled like an alley cat—old food, garbage and urine—and her grey fur would have been lovely if it wasn't matted in places and dirty. Even her claws were too long, but he noticed she was careful not to hurt him. Although she'd lived a hard life she had a kind heart. He didn't want to know how many kittens she'd had before, but she was still young herself and she carried herself like a pro. Did she want him to find a place for her kittens?

No, that's not it.

Paul silently swore. He had to be careful with his thoughts. On a certain wavelength the cats could hear them. He'd been unguarded.

What do you want? he asked.

Food would be nice.

And after that?

Water.

And after that?

Your help.

Do to what?

To save us from the dragon.

"Has she said anything more than that?" Phillipa asked Paul once he told her about their new visitor who was drinking up the water they'd put in a separate bowl for her in the kitchen, as if she'd crossed the Sahara. He'd hidden the evidence of his trip to the store, quickly stuffing it in the back of the upstairs closet, before telling her. They now sat together in the living room giving the newcomer space. "She's clearly in distress."

Stinky and dirty, Annie said with a sniff as she sauntered into the room. She jumped up onto the couch and settled beside Phillipa.

That's not nice, Phillipa scolded her.

It's true. She's sweet, though.

Paul shot Annie a look before he replied to Phillipa, "No, I don't know anything more." He didn't want to tell her that he hadn't pushed to hear anymore. In truth, he wanted to feed her and then send her on her way. Food he could do. Water was easy. Saving them from a dragon?...now that sounded like the kind of trouble he wanted to stay away from.

"What will you do now?"

He'll help her, Annie said.

Paul shot her another glance. *I didn't say I would.*

Annie just looked at him as if the answer was obvious. She knew how to get under his skin.

"She's carrying kittens."

I know, Annie said. *She told me.*

I was talking to Phillipa.

"Kittens?" Phillipa said surprised. "So you *have* to help her."

"I'll listen, that's all."

Annie licked her paw. *You don't have much time. The kittens will come soon.*

Paul didn't get a chance to reply before the newcomer came into the room.

Thank you, she said with tender politeness.

He wondered where the street cat's manners had come from. Perhaps she'd had an owner once.

We are never owned, Annie said with disgust.

He swore at her. *Keep out of my thoughts.*

When you think things like that I can't help myself and you should be more careful. She might hear you too.

He swore again, this time at himself. Annie, to his eternal annoyance, was right. Somehow he wasn't being as careful as he usually was. But there was something about this cat that unnerved him.

What's your name? he asked her.

Name?

He silently swore. She probably didn't have a name. Or a home. *Doesn't matter. This is what I can do for you. You can stay here until the kittens are born. Then that's it. I'll keep you safe from the dragon.*

No, what about the others?

What others?

The others you have to help.

"Paul," Phillipa said in a soft voice. "I don't think she's talking about herself and the kittens when she used the word 'us.'"

Yes, he was afraid of that. His heart filled with dread.

She didn't look like she had a home. So what could the problem be?

How many are there?

I have to show you. You can help us. Please.

"We can look and assess," Phillipa said.

No, that would be too close. If he took one step, he'd take more. But he was curious about the others. *Fine. Show us.*

THEY GOT in his blue Honda Civic and drove there. It was several miles away in a small subset of town surrounded by fields untouched by development. He was shocked the cat had been able to walk as far as she had. The moment Paul stepped out of the car and stared at the white split level house, fear nearly choked him, gripping his heart. No. No. No.

He looked at one of the dark windows that seemed to swallow up the sunlight instead of reflect it. There were two of them facing them like the eyes of a dead man. He shook his head. Hell no. He wasn't going in.

Please.

He didn't care how polite Lily (Phillipa had named her that and the cat didn't seem to mind) was. How needy she was. This was too much.

"I sense something bad," Phillipa said.

He sensed something worse than bad.

Paul what is it? Phillipa asked reaching him through his thoughts.

He couldn't respond. There were too many. Way too many. And the dragon...too big. Dragons like the one who owned this house scared him. There was nothing he could do. He sensed an unrelenting need, an insatiable hunger, and a suffocating love.

The dragon wasn't home, but that didn't matter. He'd briefly wondered why Lilly hadn't sent images of her problem to his mind in order to let him see everything through her eyes, but he'd thought she'd been too polite for that. However, now he knew why. She'd wanted him to experience the dragon's power himself.

When Phillipa touched his sleeve he jumped.

What is it? she asked him.

I don't deal with this. This is too much. "We'll call animal control."

"We have to go in first. We promised."

"No. I don't need to go inside. I know what's there." He turned to the car.

Phillipa blocked him. When she narrowed her gaze he felt himself shrink a little. "We've come this far. We can't turn back now."

"I don't deal with hoarders." They scared him the most. Their toxic love was frightening. Their power strong.

He looked down at Lilly who had been determined to come with them in spite of the risk. *You should have told me. I could have called animal control—*

It's not enough. You have to save us. He'll get us back. Three times he's been warned. Every time a bunch of us disappear. He cleans up and then gets more. I've survived two rounds by hiding. Come. The back door is open.

It was worse than he thought. A repeat offender? He either had a connection with the city or something bigger was going on.

The BACK DOOR led into a nightmare.

He wouldn't sleep for days. Maybe weeks.

Even before he opened the door he could smell death and negligence. He heard the sound of rustling papers, creaking furniture, overlong nails clashing against the wooden floor as cats dashed from their comfortable places to hide. It hurt too much to look. It hurt too much to see the suffering. And he tried to block their thoughts as they scattered, but he heard their panic. *Hide! Quick! Don't let them catch you! Is this another raid? Where's Lumpy? They look different.*

Paul shifted his gaze from the urine and feces sprayed on the windows and floors, to stained cups on the couch and crumbled newspapers underneath his feet. Somehow the dragon had managed to keep the smell inside the house so that it would not seep outside so that neighbors wouldn't complain. That took a massive power. He made his way down the hall, his eyes stinging from the stench.

Yes, a nightmare. It was an awful nightmare.

Oh, God, and there would be kittens. There were always kittens in situations like this. It would tear at him. He hadn't seen one yet and didn't want to. Best to leave it alone.

"What are we going to do?" Phillipa whispered.

"Run?"

"Be serious."

"I am. We leave this to the authorities."

"You heard what Lilly said. This is a pro. We have to find a way to shut him down permanently."

He felt something press against his leg. He looked down at Lilly and began to speak, but she turned away and he knew she wanted him to follow her. Which he did.

And regretted.

He regretted looking inside the battered cardboard box sitting in the center of the room.

He swallowed as he faced what he'd feared.

Kittens. Four of them. All sick. All near death. He saw a brown one move a tiny paw. *Please don't say anything,* he pleaded, hoping to keep his voice gentle. *Just stay still. Keep your energy.* The kitten turned its head to him, letting him see that one eye was crusted shut with disease. Then it opened its mouth and let out a soft, tired cry.

Kittens couldn't speak yet. They had no language of their own. But its cry said more than enough.

Its cry said "Let me live. Save me." It had given all its strength for that. As much as he wanted to he couldn't turn away.

He picked up the box.

Just as he did, through the corner of his eye, he saw something fly through the air. He felt claws against his cheek.

The sudden attack startled him so much he nearly dropped the box.

Get out! His attacker said from the coffee table. It was a mean looking cat with orange stripes. Paul had met his type before. A healthy male who'd looked like he'd been in a few fights and won them all. A dragon would know better than try to control him, a cat like him would keep the other ones in line. He could come and go as he pleased.

Lilly spoke up and told the striped cat, *He's here to help us.*

We don't need help.

It's awful here. There are better places.

You dream too much. This is the best barn that would take ones like us. I'm not leaving here.

The others should have a voice.

They're all fine. Besides, this place has an inside creek.

Old school talk. His type didn't make distinction

between a 'house', 'barn', 'creek' or 'sink' just anything that kept them warm and dry would do.

Paul understood. A stray who knew the harshness of the streets, the wildness of the forest and fields, and felt he'd found heaven inside one of the wooden barns wouldn't want that to change.

He's good to us. He doesn't try to own us like the others.

He'd stayed longer than he'd wanted and he knew arguing with the cat wouldn't help anyone. *We're leaving,* Paul said.

Better not come back, Stripes replied.

Don't listen to him, Lilly said on the drive back. *He's not like the others.*

I know.

He can be sweet when he wants to.

Paul half wondered if Stripes was the father of her kittens, but he didn't want to ask. There were plenty of others who could have held that distinction.

"You should let me look at that scratch," Phillipa said.

She'd already asked him twice and he'd ignored her. He wanted to get as far away from that house as he could. "I'm fine. It's not deep."

"It's bleeding."

"It'll heal. It wasn't a real attack. Just a warning."

"Promise to let me clean it when we get home."

He didn't argue. He also planned to take a long shower to wipe the filthy memories away.

"You must have a gift," the vet said. A woman with large teeth and too much mascara that smelled of bubblegum. "You found these kittens just in time. You've done this before."

"Hmm," Paul said, hoping to sound noncommittal. The vet didn't know what he was and he planned to keep it that way. He liked her and didn't want to have to find someone else. Lilly refused to let them take her to see the vet, but did allow Phillipa to clean and groom her.

It had been a week. The kittens were safe. Lilly was safe.

But the others weren't.

He'd barely been able to sleep because of the nightmares. He knew he had to go back. He had to face the dragon.

But how could he do it without his secret being discovered?

"Dragons have secrets too," Phillipa said as if reading his thoughts. He swallowed, facing another sleepless night as he lay in the bed beside her. He felt Annie's green eyed gaze on him as well. He hated when she looked at him like that. Urging him to act. "You're stronger with us now."

"You can't come with me," he told her. "It's only been two months, you're still recovering."

He knew Phillipa wanted to argue, but she was wise enough not to. She knew he was right. She'd only recently escaped a powerful force that had trapped her.

Her captivity had left her weak and she was only now getting back to her full power.

"Be careful," Phillipa said.

Be brave, Annie said.

THE DRAGON WAS HOME.

Paul saw the shiny black Chrysler in the driveway.

He knew he could sneak in through the back door and do a surprise attack, but doubted he would get far. Stripes would alert the dragon to any intruder and he didn't know how many of the cats were on his side. He would have to face the dragon head on.

He knocked on the solid front door that felt as hard as steel.

A weedy little man answered, large glasses hanging from a chain around his bony neck.

Somehow he'd expected that. The dragon's appearance made sense. His disguise made it very easy to fool the humans. Who would want to upset this unsuspecting, delicate, kindly looking man?

But Paul knew the man wasn't kind and he was a lot older than he seemed. He could tell by his hands. Not because they were aged, but because they seemed the strongest part of him. Everything else about the man was thin or slim, but his hands were thick with fingers like sausages.

Selfish, grasping hands. This man had perfected his grip, a skill he'd honed throughout his lives. He would hang on to what was his.

The man sighed and hunched his shoulders as if defeated. "You can't take them all," he said, turning. "You can take a few, but not all."

Paul followed him down the hall aware of how the sunlight didn't even penetrate an inch of the tiled foyer. He left the front door open, but heard it close behind him. When he turned, he saw Stripes with a catlike grin on his face.

"I've grown bored with those ones," the dragon said as he nodded to a few cats sitting on top of a dusty bookshelf, "but the others stay."

"They all need a better place."

Something dark and frightening entered his gaze, but his voice remained soft. "No."

They pay him.

That voice came from Lilly, crossing the distance that separated them. Because this house was her domain it made the telepathy between them easy. He'd told her to stay safe at home, but she'd been guiding his steps. He didn't want to hear it, but he'd suspected that there had been a bigger reason for him to be there. This weedy man wasn't just a hoarder, he was a provider. He provided cats for the lab. Not all cats were ordinary. Some were different from their species, as he was to humans. It wasn't discussed, but there was a lot of funding in trying to discover the origin of people like him and 'normal' people feared how cats and his kind could eventually outnumber humans. No one would miss any of these cats. No one would suspect the real reason this old man had them all around him and why some were cared for while others weren't.

The dragon motioned to the cats on the bookshelf again. "They are the weak ones." He met Paul's gaze and said, *I have no use for those.*

Icy fear slid down his back as he faced the challenge. The dragon hadn't opened his mouth yet had communicated with him, making it clear that he knew what Paul was. *This must end.*

By you? You think this exchange isn't lucrative enough to make sure I'm not protected? They don't want any more freaks like you. They have to understand...

They won't understand us this way.

I don't care. And I'm not afraid of you. With one call I can get you into a lot of trouble.

He was right. But Paul had learned to blend well. He could fake being perfectly normal if he had to. It was how he'd managed to survive. Fortunately, he didn't have some of the more telling signs others of his kind had—a certain shape of the eyes and ears, the sweep of their shoulders, a soft purr to the voice—that got others locked up. Or banished. Or experimented on.

Let's come to an agreement, the dragon said. *You leave quietly and I let you live.*

If you reveal my secret you'll reveal yours.

He shrugged. *I lie well. They'll believe me more than they'd believe you.*

The dragon was right. Paul didn't have his guile. A large black guy against a sweet old man? He didn't like the odds.

He studied the dragon closely. He wasn't that dangerous, just greedy and misguided. Perhaps if...

Don't fall for it, a voice said and he realized who it came from Annie.

She was always seeping into his thoughts, but she was right. He couldn't be fooled like the others. The dragon had to be defeated.

Stripes began to pace, restless, sensing the change in the air, his tail swishing. Paul felt the air grow cold, the room seemed darker. He wasn't afraid of the dark.

He leapt forward to grab him, but the dragon moved too quickly. Another move, another dodge. His reflexes were lightning fast.

The dragon smiled like a cat playing with a wounded animal before he killed it. *I'll let you live if you go away.*

Cats liked to kill for fun. Paul never did like killing things. He always had to have a reason.

This dragon was another reason why the humans didn't trust their kind. Why they'd been seen as pariahs. Why they feared them. He took pleasure in pain, in torment as much as he did with love and loyalty.

I save them, the dragon said. *Just like you.*

And then you sacrifice them.

Just the weak ones. You can't be weak in this world. You'll get eaten if you do. He made a move towards him. He knew one of them wouldn't leave the house alive. One had to dominate and one had to die.

Paul noticed three more cats had joined Stripes in his almost ritualistic pacing—back, forth, back, forth. Then he looked to his right and saw more. To his left even more. They were surrounding him. He looked at the dragon and knew he was trapped.

Now! The dragon commanded. And his followers all leapt on top of Paul, causing him to fall to the ground.

They couldn't kill him—scratch, maim, wound, yes, but not kill—he knew that much. But that didn't stop his panic as he fought against their sharp teeth and claws biting into his flesh. As he fought, the cats seemed to multiple with each swipe. He felt his energy drain away. He couldn't fight forever, there were too many of them.

Too much pain, too much sorrow, too much hunger. Too much everything. He felt himself surrendering to the darkness that seemed to permeate the house. He felt the frenzied attack slowly end and he lay motionless on the ground. He felt a weight on his chest and looked into cutting brown eyes.

I told you not to come back, Stripes said.

Get up! Get up! He knew they were all calling to him, telling him to keep fighting. Annie. Lilly. Even Phillipa. But before he could struggle to sit up he felt the grip of death around his throat. He stared up at the dragon's dark gaze. Then he felt the power of the dragon's sausage fingers draining him. Killing him. Toying with him as he did so. The dragon didn't want him to die quickly. There would be no fun in that.

Paul's eyes began to roll to the back of his head then he saw something familiar. A long haired grey cat. Lilly? Lilly! What was she doing there? How did she get there? If he died, the others would turn on her.

Stay back!

Let me help you.

She'd risk her life and her unborn kittens for him. Why? Why hadn't she listened to him?

No, he didn't care. He had to save her. A renewed rage fueled him. He looked at the dragon and went for his eyes. The dragon roared, loosened his grip and that was all Paul needed. A tiny advantage to seize his enemy's core vulnerability: His bony neck.

Paul snapped it like a chicken bone.

The dragon dropped to the ground.

Stripes hissed at him but none of the other cats moved. Some due to fear, others stayed still in mourning, others in relief.

Paul stumbled to his feet as he felt the grasping, choking energy dissipate around him. But he knew it wasn't over. He grabbed a knife and chopped off the dragon's hands. His strength.

He did the action just in time as the dragon changed shape into a sleek Persian. In his next life he couldn't take that powerful advantage with him. Paul didn't know how many lives the dragon had lived but the hands said that each one had made him stronger than the last. He hoped without them he could not do the damage that he had done in the past. The Persian sent him a cold glare before he left and his followers trailed behind him.

You're safe now, Paul told the remaining cats, some peeking out from under the worn sofa and from behind a crooked closet door. *Tell Lilly to come out of hiding. I won't be mad at her.*

Lilly isn't here, a skinny white and orange cat said.

Not there? He was certain he'd seen her. Had he imagined it?

What happens now? another cat asked.

Paul nodded at her in reassurance. *Annie knows of an*

underground network that will take care of some of you and I know of a trustworthy animal rescue that will take care of the rest. Either way someone will look after you now.

Lilly was right. She knew you would save us.

HE TOOK A LONG SHOWER. A shower so long he half expected his skin to shrivel up and drop off.

Then he slept. He didn't know for how long, but long enough not to dream. When he finally woke up, he saw a late afternoon sun peering through his window. The time said four o'clock. He shuffled into the kitchen.

About time you got up, Annie said with a sniff. *Even I don't sleep for twenty hours a day.*

He shot Phillipa a look of surprise and she smiled in return. "You were exhausted. It's been nearly two days."

"Two days!"

"The house is clear. The cats are fine."

"Where's Lilly?" he asked surprised not to see her.

She left, Annie said.

Paul's brows shot up and a feeling of hurt touched his heart. "She left without saying goodbye?"

She had bigger concerns.

Like what?

Having her kittens.

Annie yelped in surprise when Paul picked up a grape from the fruit bowl and threw it at her. He turned to Phillipa. "Where is she? Is she okay? When did she leave? How long ago was it?"

Phillipa laughed. "Don't look so worried. She's a pro. She found a nice quiet place."

"Here? Where?"

"She'll let us know when she's ready."

And when she was ready, Paul was nervous to see her. He didn't know why, but he was as he made his way inside the upstairs closet and found her with her four kittens. She looked tired but happy.

Thank you.

You're welcome. I know of a place where you and the kittens can stay and be safe.

They were right about you.

They? He didn't like knowing he had a reputation. He was about to say something more when he noticed something shiny and red behind her.

The box of chocolates! And the teddy bear. Oh no... what day was it? He glanced at his watch. February 22nd. His first Valentine's Day and he'd completely missed it.

It's a good thing you're a hero, Annie said behind him. *You're a lousy boyfriend.*

He turned and shot her a look, which she ignored, then paused when he saw Phillipa standing there. He slowly rose to his feet feeling miserable. "I'm so sorry I for—"

She didn't give him a chance to fully apologize, kissing the rest of his words away and then hugging him. "Thanks for showing me what true love looks like," she said.

"True love?"

She stepped back and nodded. "Love is helping a stranger, a mother defending her family and her friends, a man risking his life to free those in need. That kind of love is very beautiful to see."

Yes, so many types of love...all powerful, all beautiful.

Maybe one day he'd contact his parents again and tell them about Phillipa. But not yet. He hugged Phillipa back knowing that chocolates and teddy bears couldn't make this moment any sweeter. Right now he had all that he needed.

Friends, love and kept secrets.

PAWPRINTS IN THE CLOUDS

PAWPRINTS IN THE CLOUDS

PAUL GIBBONS HAD A FAVORITE ANIMAL.

It wasn't a cat.

When he opened the front door to his house and saw the dead chickadee on his doormat, one wing broken and its tiny claws up in the air, he remembered why. Walter had been there. The striped grey always liked leaving gifts. Paul had told the stubborn cat to stop, that it wasn't necessary, but the cat refused to listen.

Nothing new there. Cats rarely listened to him.

Paul sighed, grabbed a rubber glove from his hallway closet and bent to dispose of the gift, but before he could, Annie, the squashed faced black and white cat that lived with him, pounced on the dead bird and disappeared before he could stop her. He began to call out to her then changed his mind; he didn't care what she did with her stash, as long as it didn't smell. He put his glove away then looked out across his small front lawn, which was more weed than grass and soggy from a spring rain, trying to see if he could spot the gift-giver.

Walter. You have to stop this.

He waited for Walter to appear and he didn't have to wait long, the older cat came timidly up to the door. *But I need another favor,* he said.

Paul grabbed a broom and pretended to sweep the doormat. He had to be careful not to be seen focusing his attention on the cat. If anyone suspected he had a special affinity with them, his life, as he knew it, would be over. No one could know what he was. *And I told you that I've quit.*

Walter walked up to him and sat. *You can't quit.*

But he had. He promised himself. Promised her, Phillipa, his heartmate for nearly two years, the one person who made him feel less alone in a world that didn't accept people like them, and he meant to keep his promise.

Walter looked up at him hopeful. *Would you like a cardinal instead?*

Paul picked up the doormat and shook it before he set it back down. *No.*

I think I could manage a robin, but they're crafty and big.

No. No more gifts. Now go away. He walked inside and closed the door but Walter didn't stop pleading and since he could reach Paul through his thoughts the flimsy door was no barrier.

How about a frog? A chipmunk?

Paul put his broom inside the closet. *I don't want gifts and I can't help you. Find someone else.*

No one else will listen. Can you just listen?

Sure another voice said and Paul didn't need to look down and see that Annie had appeared from her hiding space and had joined him.

He frowned down at the cat. She blinked unmoved. *Listening won't hurt,* she said.

I promised Phillipa.

Phillipa isn't here.

His heart twisted with a pain that was becoming too familiar; he didn't need to be reminded of that. Perhaps listening wouldn't hurt, it would be a distraction. He needed that right now.

He sighed and opened the door. Walter walked in and said, *You've gained weight.*

Yes, he had. About fifteen pounds, he didn't need to be reminded of that either.

Walter greeted Annie before he headed to the kitchen. He'd been inside Paul's house before and treated it like a second residence instead of as a guest. He walked to the extra water and food bowl Paul kept filled just in case...

Walter took a few laps of water, his pink tongue quick and sure, and then started to eat.

Paul sighed impatient. *Did you come for a free meal?*

Give him a few seconds, Annie said, *he looks like he's come a long way.*

Paul looked at Annie surprised. It wasn't like her to be so accommodating. But then Walter did look a little beat, his ears low to his head, his fur not as full as it usually was.

Paul sat at the kitchen table and waited. He didn't

look at the cup still sitting on the counter; Phillipa would take care of it when she came back.

Walter licked his lips. *That wasn't bad.*

What do you want? Annie said.

A favor.

You already said that. What kind of favor?

I'm only listening, Paul reminded him.

I'm worried about one of the inmates, Walter said.

Walter lived with a woman and a cat named Hosta who was a therapy cat at The Horizon nursing home.

You mean residents, Paul corrected.

That's what I said.

What's wrong? Annie said before Paul could argue.

Hosta said the inmate's acting strange.

Paul shifted in his chair irritated. *What does that have to do with me?*

I need a favor.

Annie sighed. *What favor?*

Oh, didn't I say?

Paul shook his head. Annie yawned.

I need you to go see her. I think she'd like you and may be in danger. She started saying strange things and Hosta thinks they may ship her off.

Paul felt the air suddenly grow still. He knew the dangers Walter was hinting at. People like him were extra vulnerable when they got older. Some thought it was easier to manipulate them; there were even rumors that some nursing homes and rehabilitation facilities, set up specifically for those either foolish or brave enough to live openly with their difference, were really façades for labs where the humans could experiment on people like him. If that were true, this woman would never be heard from again. Like the others who have disappeared over the years.

Those like him who had an unfathomable genetic and psychic tie with cats, aka *felishums*. There were lots of myths and made up stories as to why people like him and Phillipa existed, but few knew the truth, just the outcome: A person born with the ability to communicate with cats and see life on a fourth dimensional realm.

And there was more—frighteningly so.

What do you want me to do?

Help her.

There's nothing I can do if they already suspect her. And he'd be putting himself in danger if they suspected that he and this woman were the same. There were cameras all around. They'd be watching him with her. It would be too dangerous. He'd promised Phillipa he wouldn't do that anymore. He'd act like everyone else. Try to be as normal as he could.

Phillipa won't know, Annie said. *She's not here.*

Paul gripped his hand into a fist. The cat didn't have to keep stating the obvious. *But she could come back soon and if she found out...*

He needs help.

He looked at Walter. He briefly thought of the dead chickadee that had been on his doorstep before he glanced at the single cup sitting on his kitchen counter. Someone needed help. He couldn't ignore that no matter how much he wanted to. *But there might not be anything*

I can do. Like before. He didn't want to feel that helpless feeling again. He was more afraid of trying and failing than anything else.

Just go there and see.

He would, but just to look. Nothing more.

How am I supposed to get inside? He didn't know Hosta and Walter's owner and even if he did, he wasn't reckless enough to admit that he had spoken to her cat who'd just confessed to being worried about one of the residents at The Horizon. Walter's owner was fully human not a freak like him.

You could say you're a nephew. She doesn't get a lot of visitors. They call her Mrs. Redman.

That explained a lot. It wouldn't be difficult to make her disappear. Few people would notice.

Fine.

Paul took a deep breath and then tried to see this woman with his mind's eye, trying to see her through Walter's perspective, trying to capture Walter's memories or experience of her, but since Walter had never interacted with the senior resident, Paul couldn't get a full picture of her. He got bits and pieces of information about her from Walter's conversation with Hosta, a picture of a large black shoe, a scarf, but nothing solid about the woman. The resident Hosta and Walter were worried about could be fully human for all he knew and perhaps not at risk at all. That's what he hoped for.

But he knew from experience that hoping didn't change anything.

❋

The Horizon nursing home had an elegant hardwood floor and soft pastel colored entrance that held the glamour of a hotel and the security of a prison. Paul noticed the guard at the entrance and a camera above the double doors. He walked up to the front desk of the facility and looked down at a countertop so shiny he could see his reflection in the polished wood. "I'm here to see Mrs. Redman."

The woman behind the desk wore her dark hair in a large bun. A bun so large she could hide a basketball inside and no one would suspect a thing. She looked at him and blinked. "You are here to see who?"

"Mrs. Redman. I'm her nephew."

She blinked again, this time her eyes widened, her mouth falling open in a silent O. Her expression was so comical he had to stifle a laugh as he imagined her as a cartoon character, her hair lifting her out of her chair like a helium balloon. "Really?"

He nodded and waited, careful not to look down at his reflection in the counter. He didn't want to see the man reflected there. The large, black man disguised in a false mustache, dark, square glasses and light brown hair. A man who...

He took a deep breath. He had to stay focused, not distracted. He tapped a finger against the table when he heard a faint ringing of bells. Bells? Why bells? He wanted to ask where the sound was coming from, but knew better not to ask. He'd learn that his hearing was better than most. Instead he'd stay quiet and look faintly impatient. He'd learned silence was a good weapon, he wouldn't explain. Let her make sense of his lie, it was a strategy that had worked in the past. The clerk collected herself and her manners and finally said, "I see. Well, it would be nice to let her...I mean see her have visitors."

He noticed the slip. Let her? Had they been keeping people away? Paul smiled and waited some more.

When the clerk stood he felt his tension ease. The first hurdle had been passed he was getting access. He wished he knew where all the cameras were located. If anyone was watching, he didn't want to show how relieved he felt. He followed her keeping his steps modulated so as not to draw any attention to himself. When he was being cautious he tended to creep rather than walk, that would give him away and keeping his secret was how he lived his life, how he stayed safe.

She stopped in front of a door and knocked then opened it.

The moment Paul saw Mrs. Redman he could understand the clerk's surprise that they were related. Mrs. Redman was clearly not black. She was of Asian heritage.

Walter! It had been stupid to base a plan on a cat's sensibilities.

Did you get in? Walter asked.

Paul silently swore. He'd forgotten he could connect to him from a distance. Walter was at home and Paul, in his annoyance, had opened the channel of communication unexpectedly.

You forgot to mention something, he said.

What?

She's Asian.

So? She's human, isn't she? I can't tell the difference.

He sighed. Yes, cats weren't particular about things like that. Sometimes they used neutral pronouns, which could also be a challenge. He should have known. But once Paul recovered from his shock he let himself look at the older woman more fully. He tried to see any telling characteristics that would signify her difference—a certain shape of the eyes or ears, but he didn't see anything striking. She was beautifully unattractive in a way that was endearing, with a face full of wrinkles and brown eyes as warm as roasted peanuts. Her silver hair had three streaks of black all to the left side of her face held back by a gold hair slide.

"Mrs. Redman, your nephew is here."

Paul froze. He hadn't planned that the clerk would introduce him that way. He could see the confusion on the other woman's face. What if she said she didn't have a nephew? Or didn't know him? He didn't even know the reason she was there. What if...

She smiled. "At last."

He rushed forward and took her outstretched hand so relieved he nearly fell to his knees. Another hurdle crossed; another possible disaster avoided.

The clerk nodded, her large bun bobbing, then left.

Do you need my help? she said.

He stared at her, surprised, releasing his hand from her surprisingly strong grip. Why would she ask him that? He was there to help her, but then his heart fell because he knew Hosta's concerns were right. She'd spoken without words. She was like him.

He glanced around the neat room, taking in the plush gray comforter on the bed, the tiny bookshelf that held only five books, different shaped shells, the faint scent of the ocean still lingered on them, and a picture of Mrs. Redman about twenty years younger standing on a beach with a large man of indeterminate race. *Is there a camera?*

Shouldn't be, but possibly.

Damn. That meant they were in trouble. She was likely being watched. He wanted to talk to her safe like this without words, but if someone was watching and noticed that they just stared at each other they would grow more suspicious.

Audio too?

I don't know.

Damn. He would have to assume the worst. "Aunty, it is so good to see you. You're looking good."

"Thank you."

"They are treating you well?"

"Yes." Her gaze slid over to her side table. He saw a little cat figurine, it was porcelain white with orange stripes and stood on all fours with one paw lifted from the ground as if it were set to walk away.

He lifted it surprised that it felt warm to the touch instead of cool. "It's beautiful." His heart hurt as he set it back down. The little figurine was on its own. That's how he'd spent most of his life, before Annie and Phillipa. When Phillipa came back the loneliness would end. "Doesn't it come as a pair?"

"Sometimes. I got it in San Francisco years ago."

Was that code? Was there someone in San Francisco she could be with? That California city was quite a distance away from this small Maryland town. "I'll have to take you there to get a companion sometime. Is it coming or going?"

"Depends on how you look at it. You get to choose."

"Sad to see it so lonely."

"It looks alone, but it is not alone."

He frowned, not understanding her.

There's no need to feel lonely.

He felt his heart pick up pace. How did she know? How could she tell? He wasn't alone. Not anymore, not if...

Love replaces loneliness. Focus on love.

His frown deepened. He still didn't understand her, but it didn't matter. He'd found out what he needed to. Unfortunately, he needed to find out more.

"Since you enjoy it here there's no need for you to leave," he said.

They are thinking of sending me somewhere else. "Yes, everyone treats me with such kindness."

I know, that's why I'm here to save you. "That's why we chose here."

I can save you too.

I don't need saving. He didn't want anyone to try and save him. The last person who'd saved him had...

Focus. He couldn't be distracted. *Do you know when? Next week? Not sure.* "I'm glad you did."

I'll think of something. He engaged Mrs. Redman in banal conversation, letting her share about her life with her husband, trying not to feel jealous of the years they'd had together before he passed away, then told her he hoped to see her soon.

"Will you come back to see me?" she asked.

"I'll come back and see you soon."

"I'd love that," she said. It was the word 'love' that seemed to hang in the air between them. People like them didn't use that word carelessly. She was trying to tell him something, but what mattered more was helping her either stay or escape.

PAUL SAT on the side of his bed and stared at the empty chair in the corner of his bedroom. Phillipa liked to sit in the overstuffed armchair and read. She'd always wanted a window seat, he'd promised to build her one one day. "Yes," he said aloud. "She's one of us and I have to get her out of there. What should I do?"

Why are you talking to yourself?

He looked down at Annie annoyed. Of course she would enter his bedroom when he was trying to have a private pretend conversation with Phillipa.

I wasn't talking to myself.

Yes, you were. No one's here and Walter isn't calling you.

She was too nosy and too right.

I was pretending Phillipa was here.

She jumped up on the bed. *But she's not.*

That's why it's called pretend.

Annie sat and licked her paw. *Why pretend that? What do you think? Or you could ask me.*

No, need I already know what you would say.

Then you already know what Phillipa would say.

He swore. The reasoning of a cat could be annoying. But she was also right. He knew what Phillipa would say. He also knew what he wanted to do. He wanted to help Mrs. Redman escape. He didn't know how.

And he didn't have much time. Once she was loaded into one of the vans that would transport her to another facility, getting her back would be much harder. He had to get to her before the vans came, before anyone could see him. He could take her for a walk and then disappear, but the clerk at the counter and the cameras had seen his face, even in disguise, and the fake ID he'd used would only get him so far if they felt like plastering his face far and wide as a kidnapper. Tracking him down would be difficult but not impossible. He didn't want to have to move again. He had to stay here. He had to stay here for Phillipa.

How could he make her disappear without anyone looking?

First he had to change their suspicions about her, which could give him some time. If she no longer was of any interest to anyone then that would help.

There was money in the exchange, not just scientific curiosity. He wondered what had given her away.

The Assessor comes Wednesday, Annie said.

Assessor?

Yes, she wears bells. Hosta said so.

Bells?

Yes.

A bracelet? Or earrings?

Don't know. It's noisy.

Bells...he'd heard bells when he'd visited Mrs.

Redman. The Assessor had been there. That made it important.

She was the one who made the recommendation. You could trick her.

That was too dangerous. Assessors were highly keen observers. They had methods to spot others like him. Generations ago they were given free reign and created tests that supposedly could determine a child's genetic makeup and personality propensity at birth, but after a number of misdiagnosis and public outcry, plus debunked scientific results, the scientific community realized Assessors' predictive measurements were inherently flawed as well as the data bias that had been built into the assessment instruments. The practice was cancelled after many lives were ruined. There was evidence that differences began to show themselves in individuals after different stages. Some, like him, discovered their differences at seven; others didn't see a difference until their late teens and even others by twenty or late thirties.

With the onset of different feline traits and abilities so varied, predictive analysis became more of a guessing game than true fact. They weren't called 'Assessors' anymore. They'd changed their name over fifty years ago to D2 counselors, in an effort to distance themselves from their violent past of mass killings, incarcerations, exploitations and experimentations.

But their job was the same.

After generations had suffered at the hands of Assessors, many parents like his, had learned to become extra diligent. They'd protected him as best they could, and he in turn had protected them by staying away from them.

Paul didn't meet his first Assessor until he was seven. A very nice man who smelled like tuna and honey; who wore large glasses with purple tinted lens. Paul had liked him. But he couldn't trust him, his parents warned him not to trust anyone. He couldn't show off how fast he could run, he had also taught himself not to flinch when he heard certain sounds that would make him a target.

Although predictive analysis was still in its infancy, it was still quietly used with vulnerable populations like runaways, those on a different mental developmental spectrum, addicts and the senior population. Paul had managed to outsmart them in school; but a professional would be a challenge.

A top statistician, later proven false, had spread fear by exaggerating the correlation with feline blood and criminal proclivities. Especially hinting at the power that some of them had; powers that Paul fought to keep secret. The media took the scent of a meaty story and turned it into a full course meal that, nearly a hundred years later, made his life a precarious event. But he couldn't change the mind of the public; he could only try to save his own as best he could.

But maybe saving Mrs. Redman was impossible. She didn't seem worried. Mrs. Redman had lived a long life, she had decades on him. There was nothing he could do.

You have to help her.

No I don't.

She's not coming back.

He looked at the empty armchair. That's not what he wanted to hear.

THE ASSESSOR at the nursing facility was pleasant, but they were paid to be. They were paid to be professional liars—to hide their feelings or to show no feelings at all. He'd learned that from the Assessor he'd met when he'd gotten arrested.

They watched you, but he'd also learned to watch them. He knew what they were looking for and also what they didn't see. They were very patterned based, they didn't like surprises, but his type were—like humans— very varied. Some reached full form in youth like him, others had their distinctions come when they were in their teen years and a tiny few in middle age. He felt the most sorry for them. Most had families that disowned them, their lives shattered.

But he had to be careful, Assessors were very meticulous. Saying he was a relative put him in their sights as well.

"We feel that your aunt would be better supported at another facility," the Assessor said with a pleasant smile. They sat in the office the Assessor used when she visited the facility. Her eyes were a deep blue, mesmerizing, and every time she shifted in her seat, he heard the sound of bells. Tingling bells, playful bells, charming bells...

He couldn't be distracted.

Paul cleared his throat and adjusted his glasses. "She likes it here."

"And how are you related?"

He'd already told her, but he didn't mind repeating it. "A nephew."

"We didn't realize she had family."

He waited.

"Through marriage I take it?"

He waited some more. Unless she asked a direct question he wasn't obliged to answer. Let her come to her own conclusions.

"Are you aware of the increased fees?" she asked.

"Increased fees?"

"Yes, I'm afraid her particular needs are creating an undue strain on the regular staff. Based on the contract she signed with us, unless she can afford more extensive care, she must be moved to another facility. However, if you are willing to sign for them...?"

She let the challenge hang in the air between them, he could feel her assessing his worn jeans and faded jacket. Even if he had the money, which he didn't, he couldn't sign anything. He couldn't let them look any closer at him. This meeting was risky enough, even with the disguise, false name and light film on his fingers to distort his fingerprints.

The Assessor smiled, a smile he was starting to hate, taking his silence as the answer she expected. "Then we can agree that this move is for the best."

PAUL LEFT her office and swore. She'd gotten him. They'd thought of something he hadn't—money. The meeting with the Assessor hadn't changed anything. In a few days Mrs. Redman would be out of reach. He wouldn't be able to save her.

He shoved his hands in his pockets and headed down the hall, feeling defeated. He sighed then caught his breath when he noticed a woman come from around the corner. She came down the hall from the other direction, carrying a shoe sized box in her hands.

He swore again, this time with more fear than annoyance. He knew her! What was she doing here?! She could ruin everything if she saw him. He kept his head down, hoping she'd be too busy to notice him. Most people were and the glasses and different hair color should throw her off enough to...

"Hi, what are you doing here?"

He'd keep walking, pretend he didn't see her. She'd think she'd made a mistake and then he could get out of there. To his relief she didn't follow him. He made his way outside and took a deep breath. That was too close.

He walked to his car and began to open it when someone said, "Yes, I thought it was you! I wasn't sure at first, but this car of yours is recognizable."

It was old and needed a new paint job if that's what she meant, unlike the silver electric she drove.

Paul briefly closed his eyes. He'd been *so* close. He couldn't continue to pretend to ignore her. He bit his lip then spun around. She smiled at him. Unlike the Assessor it was genuine. She had big teeth and wore too much mascara but she was a local vet he trusted and she had helped him when Annie had first shown up on his doorstep and with other cats he'd rescued. He blinked at her and pretended to look surprise. "Hi."

"You must not have seen me inside. Are you okay?"

"I have a lot on my mind." He shifted his gaze away; he found her unnerving outside of the clinic, more...human. At the clinic she seemed like someone who could help him, outside she was a threat even if she didn't intend to be.

She looked at him with concern. "I'm sorry."

He shrugged. "Do you have family here too?"

"No, I come for the birds. Some of the residents tend to about five of them. Unfortunately, they lost one." The vet looked down at the box in her hand. "I'm taking it to find out what went wrong..."

Paul was only partly listening as she spoke about what she hoped to uncover. She'd given him an idea. He kept staring at the box. She had taken the bird out of the place without anyone asking questions. That was his option. She'd helped him again.

"Good luck with that," he cut in when she took a breath. "I've really got to go."

"Is everything okay?"

"It's better now."

Mrs. Redman changed her will making her 'nephew' the executor of her estate before she died that week. The irony wasn't lost on him that she'd had to die in order to be free. The deception had to be orchestrated well, when she took the untraceable drug that would briefly stop her heart, claiming her body, without ceremony; letting her recover at his place before signing her up under a different name at another nursing home in another county without any Assessors on the premises where she could safely spend her final years.

She held his hand in the strong grip he'd grown used to, before she said goodbye. "Remember you are not alone," she said.

And Paul smiled, still not understanding her words or the worry he saw in her warm, brown eyes and wished her well.

THAT NIGHT PAUL lay in bed with his eyes closed. He then felt a rough tongue scrape against his cheek. He licked his lip and tasted tears. He hadn't even realized he'd been crying.

Why did you stay? he asked Annie.

She licked his face again without a reply.

He was glad. He didn't want to know why she'd stayed with him. He was glad she had, although the ache of loneliness threatened to consume him. He shouldn't have thought he could have a normal life, that he could have what others did. He was different, even more than others like him. He was at the highest degree of mixture, of power, of danger.

That's why he'd lost Phillipa.

He shouldn't have listened when she said she wanted to join him on a rescue mission. A cat had told them about two boys being kept in a basement. That the human was too crafty for the police. Paul had grown confident that he could safely rescue them. Phillipa thought so too. But she should have stayed home. She wasn't as strong as him. But she wanted to and...

You couldn't have stopped her.

The human was indeed crafty. Crafty enough to have a *felishum* on the premises. A large man who was more powerful than Paul had ever imagined. They'd fought and Paul was nearly defeated with the swipe of one powerful claw. The man could have killed him, if Phillipa hadn't jumped in front of him and saved Paul's life.

A life Paul didn't think was worth saving, especially one without her.

He hadn't been fast enough to stop her; fast enough to push her out of the way. He didn't hear her neck snap, just saw her body crumble to the ground. He didn't hear a scream rip from his throat.

He dispensed with the human and *felishum* quickly, but Phillipa, he held her, he whispered her name, but it was too late.

He felt her light force leave her. Begged her to stay. Wished he could exchange his life for hers.

Her gaze shifted to the two frightened boys huddled in the corner. *We saved them. It was worth it.* She met his eyes. *Don't be sad.* She told him with a soft smile.

How could she say that? He didn't get a chance to ask her before his wish was granted. He exchanged one of his lives for hers and watched her transform. Their different lives weren't just a rumor. Some did have nine lives, some less, some more. He felt a life force leave him and fill her and saw her turn into a fawn colored Abyssinian. She blinked at him with unknowing eyes, not recognizing him. He wouldn't be part of her new life. She walked away and disappeared from his life.

He still hoped she'd return. He didn't care what form she took. But the likelihood was slim.

He'd always be alone.

I'm here. Annie said.

Paul kept his eyes closed and groaned. He really had to be careful around this cat. *I wasn't talking about you.*

So you're not alone.

It's not the same.

Yes, it is.

He didn't have to be lonely. Finally Mrs. Redman's words made sense. He was alone, but the loneliness that threatened to swallow him was a choice. He could either think about his life without Phillipa or think about the nearly two years they'd had each other. Loved each other. She was still in his heart, always would be. She'd left him with a gift, one he wouldn't take for granted. She'd saved him, he wouldn't waste his life mourning her. That wasn't what she'd want.

And Annie had stayed.

He'd never had a companion like her before. His present was already different than his past. He sat up and wiped his eyes. *You're right.*

I know.

When he opened the front door the following day, to his relief, he didn't find a dead chickadee. Instead it was a little porcelain cat.

The same porcelain cat that had been on Mrs. Redman's side table. The one that looked like it was either leaving or heading somewhere.

You get to choose, she'd told him.

Paul lifted up the figurine. It felt warm as he cradled it in his hands, his heart feeling light for the first time in months. He looked up at the clouds and finally knew he was going forward in his life, and he wasn't alone.

PAWPRINTS IN THE GRASS

PAWPRINTS IN THE GRASS

THE KITTEN WAS LIMPING.

Paul Gibbons didn't particularly like cats, but he had a weakness for kittens.

A hopeless, dangerous weakness.

He didn't know what it was about them that drew him to them, made his heart go soft when he needed to keep it hard in order to survive. He thought puppies were cute as well as baby chicks.

But kittens...kittens got him every time.

So he couldn't ignore the one that was painfully limping its way towards him. Although it was several yards away he knew it was trying to reach him. He'd learned to sense that. So he waited. He didn't get up from where he was sitting on that cool spring morning in the park, quickly glancing up at the scattering of tall trees— some evergreens and others slowly sprouting pink and purple buds—before he looked at the kitten once more. He had come there to ruminate over the strange dream that had haunted him the past two days: An odd dream about a shining silver box.

He tore his gaze from the kitten and glanced behind it at an abandoned house across the strip of road that circled around the park. It had a pile of trash—old boxes, a couch, suitcases, broken chairs— in the driveway. He briefly wondered if the "For Sale" sign was a joke. He let his gaze fall to the kitten again and noticed it had made progress and was getting closer. He slowly stood to his feet and casually walked towards it, eager to meet it halfway so that it wouldn't have to limp anymore. It was a risk to do so, but one he was willing to take.

Had it been a cat he would have turned and started walking, pretending it wasn't there. It was safer that way. He'd walk to a place where they couldn't be spotted together. It took a bold cat to come up to a stranger—a human. People would notice.

Feral cats were supposed to be skittish, wary of humans. Domesticated cats had to be coaxed, but had learned (sometimes) to trust humans. Both knew Paul wasn't exactly human himself. That he was one of the others: a feared species that had an unfathomable genetic and psychic tie to cats.

It was dangerous for the world to know that. His kind had been analyzed, feared, hunted for generations.

But a kitten wouldn't know that. A kitten was too new to the world to understand all its dangers. A kitten only knew that it needed help. Its instincts led it to him.

Paul glanced around the park relieved that in the early morning there were few people to see them. The kitten was too small for anyone to see from a distance, its spotted coat hidden in the tall grass in a section that had yet to be mowed. Had the kitten been noticed by anyone, it likely would have been rescued. Scooped up in some- one's arms and rushed home.

But Paul wouldn't do that. Paul didn't want to be seen with the kitten so he would bend down and quickly scoop (hide) the kitten in his knapsack. Which was exactly what he was about to do when a jogger came up to him.

"Have you seen a purple water bottle?"

He quickly straightened, careful to not look startled or guilty, and looked around. "No, sorry."

The woman's brown gaze swept the area and he felt his pulse quicken. If she spotted the kitten that would ruin everything, he wouldn't be able to provide it with the help it needed. He stepped in front of it hoping to block her view. He was a big guy so that wasn't too hard. But he had to be careful, not because he was a black man, but because of the way he moved. The way he could move— fast and quick like lighting, with a panther's agility, which could alert suspicion. He couldn't be too nimble or smooth. He had to be subtle, barely detectable so the woman wouldn't notice. Paul knew he'd succeeded when the woman looked disappointed but not afraid. She hadn't noticed anything wrong.

"I can be such a klutz," she said, brushing the thick black braid from her shoulder. "I sat down for a drink and then..."

He shrugged. "Sorry."

"Oh well, thanks."

He nodded.

She waited.

He swallowed. What else did she want? Why wasn't she leaving?

A soft grin touched her full lips. "I've seen you around here."

"Uh...okay."

She handed him a card. "If you ever need company, don't hesitate to call."

He took her card, making sure to keep his gaze on it and not wonder why she smelled like nicotine and brown sugar. He tried (and failed) not to look at her body and wonder where she'd pulled the business card from. He didn't think tight grey yoga pants had pockets or the orange tank-top she wore. Perhaps they'd been hidden in her cleavage? Yes, there was plenty of space, *ample* space, *amazing* space there and...damn he was actually looking there. He wasn't that kind of guy; at least he didn't think he was. He tried not to be. He swiftly raised his gaze and returned her grin, hoping he looked charming and not like a creepy pervert. "Oh, 'kay."

She winked and then jogged off. He felt himself breathe again. He hadn't expected that. Women didn't usually come up to him like that. He preferred it that way. Being alone was the way he kept himself safe and those he cared about.

He tucked her number in his jeans' back pocket; he had no intention of calling her. Cute as she was. He'd noticed her too. But noticing people from a distance was what he'd gotten used to after Phillipa.

Phillipa. He took a deep steady breath, inhaled the scent of dry soil, felt the soft warmth of the sun on his bare arms. He wouldn't think about her now. He was getting better; it didn't hurt as much to think about her.

He had other things to think about now.

Paul looked down and froze. The kitten was gone.

Gone!

He swore. The woman had so distracted him he hadn't paid attention to it. Had someone else seen it and taken it? Had some wild animal grabbed it?

Had some...

Tired.

The faint voice came to him and he took a hesitant step forward and saw the kitten lying on its side with its eyes closed.

Hold on, he told the kitten, using his ability to communicate without spoken words. He quickly scooped the kitten in his knapsack ready to head to his car but in his haste he stepped on something that caused him to lose his footing. He fell forward, feeling himself descending to the ground as if in slow motion. He twisted himself so that he would fall on his side. The last thing he wanted to do was fall on a kitten—not just any kitten, an injured one—and kill it. He'd never be able to live with himself.

He hit the ground hard, but barely felt the impact. All that mattered was that the kitten was alright. He pulled the knapsack from his shoulder and peered inside, his heart pounding.

Wide green eyes stared back at him. He felt his pulse return to normal.

I fell, he said answering the kitten's silent question.

Paul looked around to see what had caused his fall and spotted a purple cyclical object. He picked it up. He'd found it. The missing water bottle.

He took it. Perhaps he'd return it to her. Perhaps he'd look at her card and remember what her name was. Perhaps he'd call her and tell her that he had it. Perhaps he'd let her take him out.

Perhaps he'd briefly gone insane because he knew he couldn't date a human no matter how cute she was.

He'd leave it on a bench or something. Right now he had bigger things to focus on.

It's okay. You're safe now.

The kitten blinked.

It was young. Possibly too young to communicate well. That would be a problem. Fortunately, he knew who could help him.

He needs a vet, Annie said when she saw the kitten. Paul sat on his couch giving the kitten water through an eye dropper not wanting to overwhelm its tiny system. Its pink tongue lapped up every drop. Paul glanced at the squashed faced cat sitting at his feet.

I already made an appointment for early tomorrow, but I thought you should talk to him first.

Why me? You found him.

He might feel more comfortable with you.

I'm not his mother.

Lucky kid.

He winced when he felt the swipe of claws bite into the flesh of his ankle. He glanced down and saw the scratch marks, but no blood. He glared at her. *What was that for?*

She casually groomed her paw as innocent as an angel. *If you want my help you have to be nice to me.*

I'm always nice to you. That's my problem. He set the kitten on the couch cushion beside him.

Annie jumped up on the couch beside Paul, walked across his lap then bent down and sniffed the newcomer.

Has he said anything? Paul asked her.

Only that he's tired.

Nothing about what he was doing there, how he hurt his foot or...

He said he was tired and then fell asleep.

For how long?

How should I know?

Is it a nap tired? Pain tired? Exhaustion tired?

He'd just tired. He needs rest. Does the rest matter?

Annie had become a habit. He'd never admit he'd gotten used to her, that at times she could be useful even, she was too conceited to flatter, but right now he wanted to shake her. He didn't like not knowing what to do, especially with something so young and vulnerable.

Take him to the vet.

I will.

Good. She jumped down from the couch then licked the wound she'd inflicted on his ankle.

It was an apology. He was willing to accept it.

That night he dreamt about the silver box again.

❄

THE VET WAS NICE. She wore too much mascara and had big teeth, but he liked her. Sometimes she smelled like strawberry bubblegum, today it was grape.

"Oh, this one is very young," she said.

Paul shoved his hands in his pockets and nodded. He'd been in this examining room enough times that he could walk around it blindfolded. But although the room was inviting with its large window that soaked up the faint rays of the morning sun, walls painted a calming blue and a row of wooden cabinets over a green colored countertop that held a weigh scale, he never let his guard down. "Hmm."

"Kind of reminds me of you." The vet looked up from the kitten and met his gaze. "A relative?"

He froze. Jokes like that weren't funny. Especially for someone like him. Did he blow it off? Pretend she hadn't said anything? Misunderstand her? Change the subject? He decided he'd be cool about it. He focused on her name plate, although he didn't need to. He knew her name. He just never felt the need to use it. He came to her with various cats. She didn't ask too many questions, which was why he liked her. She helped heal them and he paid his bill. That was the extent of their relationship.

But now he had to be a little more human to Dr. Eileen Halcort.

He lifted his gaze to meet her face. The charming smile he'd meant to use on her froze on his lips.

She knew.

She knew about him. He could see it in her eyes, smell it.

He knew that scent. It wasn't fear, but heightened awareness.

His mind raced. She could reveal his secret, tell someone her suspicions. She knew where he lived. He'd have to move again; start somewhere else where no one knew him. Perhaps that was the right thing to do. He'd been in this small Maryland town too long. He'd gotten too comfortable. He should have taken the kitten somewhere else, to another vet in another city, maybe even another state. The vet had put together a pattern over time. It had been over a year since he'd started coming to her. He'd given her plenty of evidence that his rescues weren't exactly normal.

He'd been careless. If only Phillipa hadn't…

"It's okay," she said, her voice softer then he'd ever heard it before. "I won't tell anyone."

He wouldn't nod. He wouldn't acknowledge her words then he could deny it. After this appointment he'd make sure never to see her again.

"My father's like you."

He swallowed, gripping his hand into a fist. What did that mean? Did it mean he liked to rescue animals? Or that he was *truly* like him? It was trick. It was a way to get him to reveal himself, but he couldn't trust her. He couldn't trust anyone.

Then he felt it…a soft breeze, but that was impossible. He glanced at the closed window. They were inside and there was no fan, it was too soon for the air conditioning. But he felt the breeze anyway, then he felt a soft touch, a soothing sensation before his mind filled with color—blues and light reds. What the hell was going on...?

Then he noticed her grin and realized the feeling was coming from her.

"What are you doing?" he demanded, making sure to sound angry rather than afraid.

Her eyes widened before she mouthed, "Did you feel that?"

She was doing it on purpose, why? Who was she? *What* was she? A new secret weapon to suss out his kind? He couldn't admit that she had affected him; he couldn't admit that kind of weakness.

"Just wrap his leg and send me the bill." He tried to make his voice sound as cold as possible.

She stroked the kitten, but locked her gaze with his. "It's how I calm them," she said, but he knew she wasn't referring to how she was petting the kitten, instead she was revealing something about herself and her strange ability. "I've never used it on a human before. I'd probably get along with them better if I could."

She was speaking in code, but he understood her. She'd used the word 'human.' She'd called him a human. That was a good sign, right?

"I can't communicate in their language so I developed a way to speak with touch, it's not sophisticated but it works with them." She hesitated before she said, "You can trust me."

He wanted to. He was keenly aware she was downplaying what had just happened between them, she'd used more than touch, she'd managed to fill the room with color and shift the mood of the very air around them.

The thought of her power excited him. He desperately wanted to know more. He wanted to know more about her. To trust her. It was a whisper of yearning, just like the tiny tug of lust that urged him to call the jogger. He wanted to trust the vet just so he didn't feel alone. It had been a year since Phillipa and he wanted...

He couldn't replace her. He didn't want to.

But he couldn't ignore that she'd left him with a longing, she'd made him a little greedy. He wanted to be with someone again, wanted to feel like he belonged. He wanted to honor how she'd opened up his heart and made him feel worthy of being alive instead of a freak.

But the vet had nothing like Phillipa's delicate features and pretty smile. Instead she was a handsome woman with big teeth that reminded him of canine's wolfish grin.

He wouldn't admit a thing. "You're good at what you do. So does he need any medicine?"

THE PROBLEM WAS that although the kitten's leg would heal (it was sprained not broken) it was too young to communicate what was wrong. Its language skills were very limited. The kitten only knew the words *tired, hungry, sleepy, bad,* and *scary.* And the images he sent to Paul's mind were of the inside of a box. It didn't make any sense.

Maybe there's nothing wrong, Annie said after Paul

tried another frustrating attempt to communicate with the kitten that was now sound asleep on his lap. *Just keep him or get him adopted. Kittens are easy.*

But Paul sensed something more.

It had only been five hours since the vet's visit. He didn't want to go back.

That was the last thing he wanted to do.

But Dr. Eileen said she could communicate without words.

She said her father was like him.

He didn't want to admit that he wanted to know more, but that wasn't important.

He had to get over his pride. He had to get over his fear. He had to seek her help for an entirely different reason. He felt he could trust her and he needed that right now.

He stood with the kitten cradled in one hand.

I'm coming too, Annie said following him to the door.

You're staying here. He gently put the kitten in a carrier.

Why?

Just in case it's a trap. If I'm not back...

You'll be back.

I'll leave a window open.

You'll be back. The vet's safe.

She sounded certain, but he wasn't. He could be risking it all—his life, his freedom—but for the first time in a long while, it was a risk that made him feel alive again. The kitten wasn't only a weakness. It was a tiny balm to his broken heart.

"I wasn't sure you'd come back," Dr. Eileen said as they stood in the same examining room he'd been in before. She'd led him there the moment he'd arrived after he'd called her wanting to schedule another appointment. He'd been prepared to tell her that it was urgent; that he'd wait, but she'd told him she was free and seeing the kitten again wouldn't be a problem.

The clinic was nearing closing so there were no patients in the waiting room and few staff left, but somehow the building felt as bright and airy as it had in the early morning. "I apologize if I made you uncomfortable," she said.

He didn't need her apology, just her help. "Can you... talk to him?"

She frowned. "Of course we all talk to animals in our own way."

He bit his lip hoping he hadn't misread her ability. Was she was being vague on purpose? Would she think he was crazy if he told her the truth? In his need for connection and eagerness for help, had he made a mistake? Her scent was the same; there was no fear just a calm awareness. "I think he's in trouble or someone else is, but doesn't know how to say it." He nodded to the kitten feeling awkward. "You said you have a special way with them."

"Yes, I can usually figure out where an animal is hurting. Promise you won't tell?"

He really hated her jokes. He needed her to be serious. "Hmm."

He suddenly felt that strange, but wonderful sensation again. His body felt light, his mind free...relaxed.

Was it her? How had she learned to do that? Was he in danger but felt too good to care?

He had to focus. *Focus!* He blinked his eyes multiple times before he looked at her, but she was focused on the kitten and the kitten stared up at her. Intense, they were communicating but he couldn't see anything or hear anything. That had never happened before.

Slowly the feeling ebbed, the colors faded and Paul felt like himself again.

He rubbed his eyes. "What the h—"

"Shh..." she said her voice as soft as a lullaby. "He will need some more time to heal."

He frowned. She was beginning to annoy him. He hadn't come for the kitten to heal, he needed information. He needed to know what to do. He opened his mouth to tell her that when he finally understood her vague statements. They couldn't talk there. For some reason she didn't feel it was safe. She would tell him more somewhere else.

He nodded. "Okay."

"Feed him something. He desperately needs it."

"Don't you have some cans of food I can—"

"The convenience store across the street has an excellent selection." She rattled off a particular brand.

He paused. She was telling him something. He knew the office had cat food, but she wanted him to buy some from across the street. She was sending him there for a reason. "Okay, I'll be sure to pick it up."

"Good. It's important," she said then she silently mouthed, "Wait for me."

He nodded. This should be interesting.

FIVE MINUTES later he stared at her stunned. She approached him in the pet food aisle dressed in all black —black jeans, black jacket, wearing a black baseball cap and boots. She also carried a black medical bag. Before he could ask her why she was dressed like that, she said, "Follow me."

"What did you find out?"

"I'll tell you soon. Keep walking."

"You weren't wearing black before."

"I always wear black for a rescue mission."

"What?" He followed her into the parking lot, heard the wail of a siren from a fire engine in the distance and steeled himself not to react to it.

"From what the kitten told me we don't have much time. I'll need you to drive."

"But what's going on?"

She went straight to his car. He didn't want to ask how she could distinguish which one was his despite the darkness. "I'll tell you on the way."

This was not what he was expecting. Besides, *he* usually did the rescues alone. And after Annie he didn't want to risk someone's life again. "Just tell me."

"We don't have time."

"You don't know what you're facing."

"I've done it before. Now drive."

He drove, but she didn't tell him much more, continuing to shush him, keeping her eyes closed, and telling him she had to concentrate. He glanced at the carrier in the backseat, but the kitten seemed to be sleeping—again.

He resisted the urge to pound the steering wheel. He didn't like being kept in the dark. Unfortunately, since she was fully human, unlike his kind, he couldn't try to seep into her thoughts the way he could with Phillipa. That made it even more frustrating.

Trust her.

He swore.

The vet looked at him startled. "What?"

"Nothing, sorry." *Don't do that*, he told Annie who'd entered his thoughts.

You're upset.

Shut up.

It's easy to reach you when you're upset. You can't be angry. It's dangerous.

He didn't want to admit how close their bond had become since he'd rescued her over a year ago. She knew him more than he wanted her to, but at least he wasn't alone. *I'm fine.*

Trust her.

He gripped the steering wheel and closed his thoughts. Annie was right; he had to stay in control.

He stopped trying to ask Dr. Eileen questions and instead followed her directions. He had to go on instincts not intellect.

It didn't take him long to recognize the park as they drove around the slender strip of road. The tall trees and wild grass looked more ominous cast in the darkness of evening. She directed him to an empty house with a pile of garbage in the driveway. The same house he'd seen a couple of days before with the ridiculous "For Sale" sign in the front yard. Before he put the car in park, Dr. Eileen gasped and rushed out of the car and began trying to push a brown cloth couch to the side.

He swore then followed her. "What are you—?"

"Help me move it."

"But—"

"Please."

He easily moved the couch out of the way then stared at the remainder of the trash. Paul turned to her and saw the vet with her hands pressed together. "There's too much. I don't know what to do."

"Tell me what's going on now."

"She's inside."

"Who's inside?"

"*She's inside*, that's what he told me. That they hid her."

Paul looked around to see where people would hide kittens and spotted a silver colored suitcase. He grabbed its handle and pulled it from the pile. He set it on the ground.

Eileen shoved him aside and struggled to unzip it, but it wouldn't budge.

He gently pushed her aside before he opened it. He jumped back when he saw what was inside.

He was expecting kittens. Maybe a cat. Not this.

Not a tiny child of perhaps two or three years of age.

Eileen rushed forward and checked its pulse.

Paul held his breath. "Is it?"

"She's alive."

"We need to call—"

"Get her back to the car. I have something to keep her going."

No police. That was usually his thing, but he was surprised to hear it from her and she responded like a pro. She said she'd done this before and he believed her. He started to walk back to the car then paused when he saw the picture of the real estate agent on the "For Sale" sign. It was the woman from the park. The one who'd lost her water bottle. Any thoughts of calling her vanished from his mind.

He watched Eileen place the child in the backseat and administer a line of fluid in her tiny vein like she'd done it before. He wouldn't ask questions.

"I can't believe she survived this. Who would do this?"

"She's like you," the vet said in a grim tone.

He didn't want to ask how she knew. Not yet.

"Take her to my place."

Her place wasn't what he'd expected and yet it was. More modern in style than his and in a pricier neighborhood. It smelled like fresh lemons and a hint of roses. It felt like the home of a successful professional, not someone who'd had to cobble together the semblance of a normal life like he had. Her existence didn't put her family in danger, like his did. He wasn't sure when he'd risk seeing his parents again. When he'd risk loving again after losing Phillipa.

Dr. Eileen set the kitten's carrier on the ground before she directed him to a room on the second level, telling him she'd be right there. As he climbed the curving staircase he overheard her on the phone making an order from a pizza delivery place that didn't exist. A place he'd called for help with his rescues. He didn't think any human knew about them.

Trust her, he remembered Annie telling him. He felt some of the tension within him ease although he still had many questions. But it felt good to trust someone again.

He carried the child and placed her on the bed in the guest room then he retrieved the kitten and placed it beside her. He stood back and stared at the pair in awe. The child looked almost as small as the kitten that snuggled up at her back as they both slept in the large queen sized bed. She was a throwaway. Some parents, who didn't know what to do with a child that manifested certain features early, got rid of their shame.

He saw the slight curve of the ears, the shape of the eyes, but those weren't reliable proof that she was *felishum*. It was more myth than reality, but it hadn't been easily dampened, especially to skittish people who didn't understand them. Unfortunately, he could sense the child wasn't fully human, like him. She'd have to grow her hair long and perhaps wear makeup to disguise her difference or find a place that would accept her. It wouldn't be easy. He'd been lucky that nothing about his physical build gave him away.

"Thank you," Dr. Eileen said.

Paul spun around to face her, surprised he hadn't heard her enter the room. That wasn't like him, he was usually more aware of his environment. He took a step towards the bed wondering if he should really trust her. If the strange sensation she'd made him feel in the clinic was even more powerful here. Perhaps it was still a trap, perhaps what he'd heard on the phone was all in his mind perhaps...

Trust her...

This time the voice wasn't Annie's. It was Phillipa's. His heart remembered her voice and it sent him the soft echo of her words now. Phillipa, whose love and kindness had slowly gotten him out of his shell. Phillipa, who had taught him that the world didn't have to be a cold, lonely place; a woman he'd loved and had risked her life for him.

He took a deep breath, steeling himself against remembered joy and pain.

He had to trust that his instincts weren't wrong, that she wasn't a threat. "What did you say?" He knew what she'd said, but he wanted to fill the silence.

A faint smile touched the corner of her mouth. "Aren't you going to ask me what I'm going to do?"

"I don't think you'll tell me."

She nodded. "Maybe another time."

At least he was beginning to understand her a little; she liked to share as little about herself as he did. "How did you get involved in rescues?"

She paused before she said, "You're not the only one with secrets in this world."

He flexed his hand, somehow that felt good to know.

"Thank you," she said.

Paul folded his arms wondering if she was patronizing him. He hadn't done anything. There hadn't been anyone to fight—no shifters to slay, no dragons to kill; he'd just moved a couple of items. "You've already said that."

"I need you to understand how much I mean it. I wouldn't have found her in that mess."

"But you did."

She shook her head. "No, you did. You went right to the correct suitcase."

"It was the only one there."

"No, there were at least five others."

He hadn't seen them. He only saw one. The silver suitcase. The one that reminded him of his dream...

Dr. Eileen started to smile. "Oh, so he did tell you," she said.

"Tell me what?"

"He told you what suitcase to look for."

The kitten hadn't told him anything. All he remembered was a silver box on the floor...that was it. That was the flash of communication—through his dream. He hadn't noticed that ability before.

Her smile widened. The smile should have frightened him. She did have large teeth—strong and white with sharp canines—but somehow he found her smile strangely...attractive. "Your powers are quite unique."

He wouldn't admit a thing. He headed to the door. "I should go."

"Thanks for trusting me."

He paused at the door then slowly turned to her. He had too many questions, but one would haunt him the rest of the night if he didn't figure out the answer.

"How...how did you know about me? What gave me away?"

She shook her head. "Relax, Paul. Nothing gave you away. You're good at blending in. I had no idea."

"Then how did you suspect?"

"Can't you guess?" When he shook his head, she glanced at the curled up ball of fur on the bed before she winked at him. "A little kitten told me."

PAWPRINTS ON THE ROOF

PAWPRINTS ON THE ROOF

To Paul Gibbons cats meant trouble. It didn't help that he lived with one.

You need a tree, the cat said.

He wasn't getting a Christmas tree. He wasn't getting any decorations. He was going to let the day pass as if it were like any other. Nothing special.

He stared out his living room window at the powder of untouched snow that covered his front yard, just enough to leave the tips of the green grass visible underneath.

Stringed lights on the house across the street, dotted the darkening sky; a large lit, ivory white snowman stood in another yard. A silent, barely detectable, breeze caused it to sway; giving the eerie illusion that it was alive. As if its curved black smile would suddenly open up and speak.

The thought made him shiver. He didn't want another Christmas season of holiday songs, holiday movies, holiday lights, gifts, candy cane spiked anything, cocoa with marshmallows, or holiday cartoons. He didn't want to endure the scent of peppermint, pine or nutmeg.

If he could close his eyes and go to sleep and wake up when Christmas was over, he would.

Anything so he wouldn't have to face Christmas *this* year. He'd once looked forward to the holiday season after years of dreading it, and if things had turned out different, he may have looked forward to this one.

But things weren't different.

Nothing had changed.

He was alone again.

You're not alone.

Paul groaned and looked over at the squashed faced black and white cat reclined like a pampered deity on his brown sofa. The arrogant, opinionated creature who'd intruded on his solitude. His life. His peace.

You're not alone, the cat said again, this time more insistent with a matter-of-fact practicality that grated on his nerves.

Paul sighed. The cat was, annoyingly, right. He wasn't alone. He had her. If nothing else, she was a reminder of the gift his girlfriend, Phillipa, had left behind. Plus memories. So many wonderful memories.

He glanced back out the window at the orange haze settling over the lawn. Something was odd about the sunset. He couldn't figure out what.

I need a tree, the cat said.

You're not getting a tree.

With shiny orbs.

You're not getting a tree.

And tall enough to climb. And sturdy. Don't forget sturdy.

Paul turned away from the strange sense of unease but it followed him over to the couch. Even as he sank into the soft cushions he felt no comfort.

What was this feeling of dread?

He glanced at the black mantelpiece and stared at the Christmas card from his parents. He put it out every year. One he'd received long ago. He hadn't told them where he was. He had considered writing them and telling them about Phillipa and her untimely death. But there was no point now. Her death made it clear it was best to be alone and keep those he cared about safe.

Also, he feared he'd see guilt in their eyes. They loved him and blamed themselves for what the world saw him as—a freak.

A genetic abnormality no one could figure out. There hadn't been others like him in the family line. They'd both been vetted carefully to make sure such an occurrence could never happen.

But it had. There was still so much science didn't know about abnormalities like him.

A felishum: a person with a strange genetic and psychic tie to cats. He could communicate with them and see things in a fourth dimensional world. And there was more but he was only starting to discover the new depths.

Children like him usually broke up marriages. One or both partners might blame the other (even suspecting the other had been unfaithful). But his parents had bonded even closer. Both were determined to protect their son.

And it had worked, for a while, until Paul

started getting into trouble. Solving cases and helping people in ways he shouldn't have been able to. By his teens he'd caught the eye of law enforcement, too frequently to be safe. So he travelled.

Distance kept them safe. They'd guarded him, keeping his true nature secret, allowing him to reach adulthood unscathed, and he'd protect them in return.

He didn't stay in one place too long. This small Maryland town bordered by hills that thought they were mountains, had been his longest stay so far. More than three years. He hoped to remain unnoticed. It was easy to stay away from people here.

He'd made it through another year with his secret safe, money in the bank and a roof over his head.

He would not be captured or studied or sent to live in designated areas with "his own kind," which were usually located in crowded cities or sometimes in rural places with no zip codes or government support.

Some managed to live with humans in a tenuous harmony, but those areas were still more experimental than accepted.

There were also specific districts were felishums lived that catered to humans with a particular sexual interest.

Paul knew individuals who managed those districts profited off of a very lucrative business, but he had no desire to enter that type of enterprise. Other, more mercenary felishum types, used human's petty differences, like ancestry (which was the easiest to exploit), to their advantage, choosing to fight in certain wars for whichever side paid best. There was power in fear and division.

Of course there was another more dangerous way to exist. The way of powerful felishums who made humans nervous, but Paul would only choose that option if truly desperate.

He wouldn't become that desperate.

Desperation came with bad planning. He'd been living this way too long to know that planning meant the difference between life and death.

He was lucky.

He'd not take that for granted. Someone like him never could.

I'm heeeereee.

Paul looked up at the ceiling and frowned. *I know you're here.*

But you're brooding and locking me out.

Yes.

The cat climbed onto his lap and settled there.

Paul sighed. *You have all this space on the sofa and you have to sleep on me?*

You're no different than the sofa.

Paul wasn't sure whether the cat was referring to the fact that he and the sofa were both big, brown and a little worn or something else. He didn't care to ask.

We should go to the vet.

We're not going to the vet. Paul folded his arms. Annie was the only cat he knew who enjoyed going to the vet. But it wasn't for checkups. It was the veterinarian, Dr. Eileen Halcort, who intrigued her. But Paul knew he had to keep his distance. Although Dr. Eileen hadn't told anyone about his secret, had shared that her father was like him, and he knew she had a few secrets of her own, he didn't trust that he could get close to her.

Because getting close meant loss and he didn't want to feel that again.

They'd worked well together—once.

Once was enough.

Life was good. He had three days before Christmas then it'd be over and he could look forward to another year.

Annie yawned wide, showing off her sharp, white teeth before she stood up, stretched. *There's someone at the door.*

No one is at the door.

You'll hear them soon.

No one is coming.

They're going to ring in a minute.

*No, they...*Paul silently swore when the sound of the doorbell interrupted his thought. How did the cat know they'd ring and not knock?

Because I'm special.

He swore. He should have blocked her from hearing that. He'd gotten careless. It was likely the sudden unease. He didn't like visitors.

And he hadn't ordered a delivery.

He looked through the peephole and saw nothing.

Strange.

He turned away.

The moment he sat down the doorbell rang again.

What the hell?

He opened the door.

Gasped.

Not at the sight of the well-dressed black woman in the grey wool coat who stared at him wide-eyed, but at the orange haze behind her. It seemed thicker somehow, and the air didn't smell the same. The air felt cool but not cold. It should be cold.

He glanced at the snowman that continued to sway, the orange haze making it look like it was a stack of three pumpkins instead of snow. Pumpkins made him think of jack-o-lanterns and ghosts and dark creatures. The snowman's smile turned strangely sinister.

Paul didn't move from the doorway, relieved that the woman wasn't a stranger, but unable to release a growing unease. "Do you see that?"

"See what?" Dr. Eileen said.

He finally looked at her. "That the sky's different?"

She blinked at him. At times it surprised him she could blink at all, considering the amount of mascara that blackened and thickened her lashes. He inwardly groaned. Of course she wouldn't see anything different. She was nothing like Phillipa. She was just a regular human.

A human with a certain gift of her own, but he didn't want to get close and ask too much about it. If she didn't see anything then he could pretend he didn't see it either.

He rubbed his eyes. "Sorry. It's nothing. Never mind." He rested his hands on his hips. "So what's this game you're playing?"

"Game?"

He nodded.

She frowned. "I wasn't playing a game."

"You rang the doorbell then ran off."

Her frown increased but Paul didn't notice it as much as her sharpened gaze. Never a good sign. That meant he'd screwed up somehow. "I just arrived. I didn't get a chance to ring the bell."

He felt his stomach twist. "Really?"

"Yes, do you think I have time for childish pranks?"

"No."

"Can I come in?"

"Do you have to?"

She opened up her coat and the inside pocket revealed the head of a kitten.

Paul swore. A spotted brown and black kitten. Why did it have to be a kitten? Why did she have to know they were his weakness? He had to get over it.

Unfortunately, it wouldn't be today.

He took one last look at the strange orange haze, now tinged with a sickly green and streaks of blood red, before he motioned her inside. "What is it?"

She walked passed him, the scent of bubblegum clinging to her. Thankfully, not peppermint but watermelon. She cast a wary look at his couch then decided to sit in the armchair.

A bold move. He didn't like sharing his armchair. Before he could persuade her to move she said, "Another child is missing."

"Listen, what happened last time was just a fluke."

"No it wasn't. I wouldn't have come here if I had other options. Trust me. We need your help." She motioned to the kitten.

Paul considered his next move. He could pull her out

of the chair and guide her to the sofa. It would be a bit awkward but doable. Or he could try to persuade her to leave. "You don't need my help. You're better off without me."

She leaned back. "No need to be modest."

"I'm not. I'm being practical." Why did she have to look so damn comfortable sitting there when he felt every part of his being on edge? "I didn't have any special dreams so I'm not sure I'll be of any use to you."

He hadn't had any dreams lately, which felt strange. Especially after thinking he'd gained a new power after saving a child from being thrown away, but now he wondered if it had been anything at all.

Dr. Eileen pulled the kitten out of the inside pocket and set it on the ground.

It was possibly the smallest kitten he'd ever seen. "Should it be away from its mother?"

"Yes, it's old enough."

Annie sniffed the new arrival and said, *A runt from a litter of seven I'd say.*

I'm not a runt, the kitten said annoyed.

Face the facts. I've seen crickets bigger than you.

No you haven't.

Leave it alone, Paul warned her. *This is serious. It's scared.*

I'm not scared, the kitten said. *I'm really really scared.*

So it was old enough to communicate but not with a precise vocabulary yet. That didn't give him much to work with, but it was better than nothing.

"Something warm to drink would be nice."

Paul blinked. A voice. A voice outside his head. It wasn't the kitten and it wasn't Annie.

He swore, returning his gaze to Dr. Eileen. He'd briefly forgotten she was there. Unlike Phillipa, he couldn't read her thoughts. Instead he'd have to resort to reading her face—a pinched mouth hiding what he knew to be big teeth, her ankles crossed—not primly but tense. He tuned into her scent, she smelled like someone on high alert. She was worried.

Her pointed criticism made it clear he was being a terrible host. Fair enough. He wasn't used to hosting people. He wanted to tell her to leave the kitten with him for a couple hours and then come back later, but he couldn't risk upsetting her. He hated that his safety remained in her hands.

"Water, tea or cider?" he said, trying his best to sound cordial instead of impatient.

"No coffee?"

"I would have offered coffee if I had it. It's water, tea or cider."

"Not even cocoa? I'm kidding," she said waving her hand when he scowled.

You do have cocoa, Annie said.

I'm not giving her cocoa.

Phillipa can't drink it so...

Paul turned to the kitchen. "I'll get you tea."

"What kind do you have?" Dr. Eileen asked.

"The kind that you boil in water."

His manners were awful, but he didn't want her there. He needed his space. His peace. Three days before

Christmas. He had to make it until then. He had to avoid cats and Christmas. That was the plan.

And so far he was failing.

"WHAT'S THE PROBLEM?" he asked, handing Dr. Eileen black tea with cream and three sugars.

"The Yule Cat."

Paul bit his lip. He wouldn't laugh because she looked serious. Instead he looked at the kitten that was now sniffing the side of the coffee table. He took a seat, schooling his feature, being careful not to smile. "The giant fluffy one with sharp whiskers that towers over buildings?" he said, trying to mimic her grave tone.

"Yes."

"The Icelandic monster feline that only attacks people who don't get new clothes?"

"Yes."

He leaned back. "You can relax. It doesn't exist."

"I think it does."

Paul nodded slowly. "Along with Santa Claus and the Easter Bunny and Freyja and her flying cats. A particular favorite of mine," he said referring to the Norse god with fondness.

"I'm not kidding."

He sighed. If he didn't feel so tired he might find this amusing.

As a child, when he'd still allowed himself to have friends, he remembered a friend's father telling them about the mysterious Yule Cat. The man's crystal blue eyes holding Paul captive as his soft baritone lured him into the terrifying tale of the large cat that roamed the snowy countryside looking for victims. He remembered the feeling of goose bumps skittering up and down his arm. And he'd wanted to hear the story again and again, always making sure that his parents bought him new socks for Christmas just in case.

But he was over that now. There were strange, awful dangers in life. He didn't need to find them in fables and fairytales.

But Dr. Eileen was usually a sensible person. He'd listen.

"What proof do you have?"

"Children have gone missing." She pointed to the kitten. "That was once a child."

Paul surged to his feet. "No! No way. We're not going there."

"Please hear me out."

No, it was beyond reason. He'd seen many things. He'd seen cats change form, he'd seen waves of power the human world couldn't see, he'd seen felishums like him disappear like clouds—there were tales that some came back as cats without memories but that hadn't been veri-fied. Even cats were rumored to exchange a life price with powerful felishums for a chance to become human. Or at least an illusion of one. But not children. A powerful being turning children into kittens? Ridiculous.

Children didn't turn into kittens, children didn't have extra lives. If they lost one, they disappeared.

Dr. Eileen sighed. "I know it sounds strange—"

"It's not strange. It's impossible."

"Many would say your very existence should be impossible."

She might have a point, Annie said.

I'm not talking to you.

At least listen.

He didn't want to listen. Listening meant he'd have to get involved and he didn't want to. Not so soon to...why now? Why hadn't she come before Thanksgiving or after Halloween or even New Year's? And the Yule Cat? Really? He was supposed to believe in a fairy tale?

Dr. Eileen shook her head. "I can't believe someone like you would be close minded."

"Someone like me?" Yes, spell it out lady. Call me a freak. Call me all the other names my kind are called. Feel superior and then get the hell out of my life.

"You understand that there's a dark underbelly to this world."

He paused. He hadn't expected her to say that. And she wasn't looking at him as he'd feared most people would after discovering the truth about him. He felt himself weakening. Damn, he would probably end up helping.

He sat down. "First of all, the pattern doesn't fit. According to the *stories,*" he said emphasizing the word, "the Yule Cat murders children. It doesn't transform them. This kitten wouldn't be alive. Second, there have been no sightings of the Yule Cat this side of the Atlantic or in this century."

It has glowing eyes and sharp whiskers, the kitten said.

So the story goes.

This isn't a story. It's huugge.

Look at the size of you. You'd think a chestnut was gargantuan.

Hey!

Listen to the vet, Annie said. *And the runt.*

"*Me. Child. Child. Me,*" the kitten said.

The kitten was lying. But her fear was real.

Paul felt the energy in the room change, the colors shifted—expanding then contracting then expanding again before rising and falling like undulating waves. He gripped the arm on the sofa.

"What are you doing?" he asked Dr. Eileen, knowing she was the cause of the sudden change.

"The kitten's afraid."

So she sensed it too. Of course she would. That was why she was here...that was how she calmed and communicated with the animals she helped...but...

"I'm sorry. I forgot about how shifting the energy in the atmosphere can affect you. Should I stop?"

He wanted to say yes, but strangely, as odd and terrifying as it felt to feel as if he'd fallen into a semi dream state, it made things clear. The orange hue outside the window no longer looked like a vaporous smoke but seemed to start taking form.

"No, I'm fine." Paul swallowed, cleared his throat. He was starting to feel scared too, but that was a good thing. If something was wrong he needed to face it. "Keep going."

The colors came to life again and the unease spilled over his body in a cascade of sensations. Suddenly he was in a tunnel and he realized he was seeing things through the kitten's eyes.

Then he was in a room with a row of windows, but the room still seemed dark, needing the light of standing lamps, although the sun shone outside.

The room was brightly decorated with holly, decorative fairy lights, the scent of pain.

Pain?

No, that had to be wrong. The room was such a beautiful sight. It should smell like licorice and the dreaded peppermint, too much sugar, wrapping paper not...

The stench of days old sweat, pain...fear.

His heart clenched. This place...where was this place? He heard footsteps, soft voices, "I got one."

He now saw three children in the room with a jar of crickets. One child with big brown eyes looked at the kitten. And he, through the kitten's eyes, gazed back and felt no fear, only affection. "Almost enough for all of us," one of the children said.

They were eating crickets. Why were they eating crickets?

Crickets are delicious.

Shut up Annie.

The children were thin, their clothes worn.

Footsteps again. These ones heavier. Louder. A signal of danger. Someone was coming.

The crickets were quickly hidden under a dark red sofa, the stench of pain increasing.

Pain, why pain? The fear he could grasp, but where was the pain coming from? Hunger? An illness?

Something was dead.

No, dying. That was it.

Perhaps the kitten was too young to grasp that because Paul couldn't find the source in the room.

But before he could pull away from the kitten's memory he saw a large face appear outside the window and he saw large eyes.

Terrifying large eyes.

And dark whiskers.

He jumped up, startling Dr. Eileen.

"What is it?"

Paul opened his mouth but no words emerged. What he'd seen and experienced went beyond words. He needed a moment to process it. "Give me a minute," he said then left the room.

HE STOOD in front of the bathroom mirror and splashed hot water on his face. He preferred it to cold water. Helped him to think.

He couldn't figure out what he'd seen. What was going on? A connection to a kitten had never happened like that before. But now he understood the kitten hadn't been lying, Dr. Eileen had misunderstood the kitten once being a child. There were children living like wild animals, existing on crickets and who knew what else. Because they cared for her, the kitten saw no distinction between her and them. They were family.

Monstrously large eyes flashed in his mind, causing his body to tremble.

He splashed more water on his face. Winced at the pain it caused.

He couldn't be afraid. He wouldn't believe in folk and fairy tales.

No, no he must not interpret what he'd seen from the kitten's viewpoint. He had to filter it from his own.

He returned to the living room. "I'm sorry."

Dr. Eileen bit her lip before she sighed and said, "It's bad, isn't it?"

Paul slowly sat. Gripped his hands together. "It usually is."

"Is it the Yule Cat?"

His mind refused to believe it but the vision... "I don't know. I have to try again with your help." Dr. Eileen nodded in understanding.

He glanced at the kitten. *Sorry little one, but let me see it one more time.*

He steeled himself, the energy in the room shifting again allowing him to enter the memory.

He tried not to be distracted by the smells, the sight of a bony knee peeking out of worn blue jeans. Something was wrong with this room.

Then he saw it.

The windows. The sun shone bright, but it cast no shadows. Because they weren't windows. They had the appearance of them but they were really a large screen and on the other side was an observer.

He still saw terrifying eyes. But now he saw the whiskers of a man instead of a cat.

A man with silver hair coming out of his ears and a dark spiky beard and the children were his lab rats.

Paul pulled himself out of the memory and took a deep breath. "It's not the Yule Cat. But it is a monster. Possibly two." The heavy footsteps he'd heard came from someone else. "We have to organize a rescue."

He opened the front door. The orange hue was gone, the snowman no longer swayed, darkness swept away all remnants of what he'd seen.

He closed the door and returned to the kitten who sat fixed next to one of the legs of the coffee table.

Shaking.

I'm sorry. He told the kitten in earnest, ashamed by how dismissive he'd been. *You're very brave. I'm glad you came to me.*

The shaking stopped. Their eyes met.

A rush of trust. Affection. Devotion.

Very brave, he repeated in case the kitten didn't believe him. Paul crouched down, stroked the kitten's back and it began to purr and he listened as it told him more then finally he told the kitten, *You do not have to go back there.*

But the others.

We'll see what we can do.

He returned to his seat and looked at Dr. Eileen. "Tell me what you know. How did she find you?"

"She didn't. They brought her to me."

"They?"

"Yes, a sweet-looking, middle aged couple found her in their car's exhaust pipe trying to keep warm. They were relieved that they hadn't turned the car on."

It sounded like a plausible story. Unfortunately, he knew it was a lie.

There was an open vent on the roof of the house, that's how the kitten had made her way in. The residents hadn't known she was there until they spotted her with one of the children.

"What were they like? The couple?"

Dr. Eileen stiffened. "What do you mean?"

"I'm just curious. Sweet-looking doesn't tell me much."

She thought for a moment then shrugged. "Nothing stood out about them. They were friendly. The man seemed shy, the woman was the one who did all the talking. Kept telling me how relieved she was that she hadn't killed the kitten."

"And they didn't want to keep the kitten for one of their children?"

"Children?" Dr. Eileen frowned. "They don't have children."

"Yes, they do."

"No, we must be getting things confused. The kitten ran away from a place that frightened it and tried to get warm inside the exhaust of some strange car."

"No, the kitten was put there. It had been living in the house. It was fine. It could get into the house through the vent in the roof. There was no reason to run away."

"But who would put it in there? And then why save it?"

"From what I can gather, they wanted to punish the children but the cries of the cat as they tried to shove her into the exhaust alerted someone, possibly a neighbor, who saw what they were doing and thought they were rescuing the kitten, so they had to pretend and follow along."

Dr. Eileen covered her mouth. "I can't believe I got this so wrong."

"It's okay. You're dealing with a very twisted pair."

"What are we going to do?"

Damn, did he really have to go there? That seemed the best plan of action. But why the scent of pain and death in such a festive looking place?

There was something the kitten couldn't see. She was too young to see the true ugliness in the fourth dimensional realm.

But he could.

"I'm not sure yet."

THAT NIGHT PAUL HAD A DREAM. He saw the room and the children. But then he heard something.

Drip.

Drip.

Drip.

His heart lifted. A piece to the puzzle. A way to get in.

They had a leaking pipe. They'd need a plumber.

He'd offer them a surprise discount.

He contacted Dr. Eileen the following morning and told her his plan.

THE COUPLE DID LOOK ORDINARY. Too ordinary. As did their grey, two level colonial, which was so blandly normal Paul had nearly missed it along the two lane road.

It hadn't been hard to get pass the couple's initial surprise and natural defenses when he pretended to arrive at the wrong house and told them how he'd come all the way there two days before Christmas, even though he should have finished up his holiday shopping for his four year old twins.

He spoke, rubbing his hands together as if he were colder than he really was, trying not to stare at the sprawling, leafless tree at the side of the house where a large branch, knotted like a bony finger, pointed to the vent the kitten had used to enter the house.

They took pity on him and led him to the vast basement where a leaky basin stood.

In the heart of their observation room.

There were screens—both vertical and horizontal, some as big as a concert poster others as large as a bus stop billboard—everywhere, two keyboards and a long desk with two comfortable chairs for them to sit in and stare at the screens for hours.

From this viewpoint he saw how much the children's room wasn't real. The children were part of an experiment of some sort.

The scent of peppermint and pine couldn't mask the smell of decay.

He still didn't know where it was coming from.

He couldn't show his surprise. Or his disgust. But he couldn't pretend that he hadn't seen all the technology.

Instead he gave a low whistle in amazement. "Quite a set up you've got here. You doctors or something?"

"Or something," the woman said, studying him closely.

He briefly glanced at the screens like the simple tradesman he'd wanted them to believe he was. It was dangerous to linger on one image too long. Instead he looked at the basin and set his burlap tool bag down (with a loud clatter that made the man flinch) ready to get to work. "This shouldn't take long."

He watched them out of the corner of his eye.

Anger, hatred, revenge. It reeked from their pores.

He saw it in their movements. They were like him. Those who could hide in plain sight.

Did they recognize him too? Was that why they'd led him here?

What were they testing? What were they seeking to find out?

Then he understood.

They had lived cruel lives. They'd suffered at the hands of others. Perhaps they'd been experimented on. They'd been used and abandoned. They'd escaped and changed their names and mannerisms to go undetected.

But they were on a mission. The holidays made it possible.

It could be a very dangerous season.

Paul began to hum. It was a way to calm his overactive senses. He was taking in too much information.

This time of year, full of commercially manufactured cheer, could bring out the worst in people, could highlight loneliness, isolation, depression, greed, despair. Allow the worst of all living creatures to run rampant.

He dealt with the lingering sadness and loneliness of his plight but he had Annie and the memory of Phillipa to keep him from bitterness. He tried not to think about the life he could have lived if things had been different. If he'd been born different or lived in a different world. He tried not to think of his anger. He dare not call it rage. Sometimes it was best not to name things.

But he could be like them if...

Paul pushed the thought from his mind. No, never. He'd never be so depraved to seek out pain and feast on it no matter how much he was hurting. Or how much power it could give him.

This had to stop.

But how?

Did you want one of your own?

He blinked. He wouldn't respond to the woman's question. He had to pretend ignorance.

He doesn't understand, the man said. *He's not one of us. He's too big and clumsy.*

I'm not so sure, the woman said. *Watch him.*

Paul kept his gaze lowered. He couldn't react yet. He'd never dealt with two before. She spoke to him without looking at him. Her tone sweetly conversational as if she were talking about a lovely spring afternoon.

You can have anyone you want. Do whatever you want. Take revenge, fulfill desires.

His stomach roiled as she continued to talk about depraved and disgusting things.

So many different types of predators.

Children were the easiest prey, especially those no one wanted. The ones too old to be cute anymore, the ones everyone saw as someone else's problem.

The kitten had first lived on the streets where a large community had formed. No wonder there had been no alert. A street kid disappearing went undetected. This couple knew that. They exploited that truth.

So many children went missing.

He now understood why the sky had looked different. The orange hue that no human could see was evidence of a growing apathy. A protective numbness, a willing blindness so that everyone could stay safe in their homes separated from one another instead of uniting as one.

Not the Yule Cat story, but close.

"It's fixed," he said.

The woman blinked. Surprised. He knew she'd felt so certain about him. Paul smiled at her confusion and she smiled back as if she were flirting and he kept his smile in place as if he were flirting back and not picturing snapping her neck.

"Thank you," the man said.

Paul bent down, pretending to pick up his tool bag, he knew he had to move quickly.

Something whizzed by him, exploded against the wall. He flattened himself on the ground and rolled under the desk. There was a third presence. And he wasn't used to guns.

Only humans used guns.

"You missed," the woman said.

"I'm sorry."

It was the voice of a child. They had given a child a gun and the instructions to kill. Stripping it of all innocence. That angered him more than their elaborate cage and strange experiment. He hadn't seen this child in the kitten's memories. It must have been kept out of view.

They were destroyers. All he could do was protect, but he'd learned not to see that as a weakness.

Their power reached out and seized him from both sides. He felt the burning heat of tearing flesh. They kept him pinned to the cold ground, trapped, immobile under the desk. With one shot to the head the child with reddish brown hair pulled into a ponytail and chocolate colored freckles scattered across her nose, could finish him.

You have to kill them all, a voice said. It sounded too panicked to be Annie's, too certain to be the kitten's— definitely not Dr. Eileen's. But something had entered his mind. A voice he couldn't obey.

The child seemed in a daze. The hand that held the gun shook. The monsters didn't notice.

No, Paul said, *not the child.*

The child is theirs, the unfamiliar voice said. *It's lost.*

The pain increased, they could destroy him.

Kill them all.

The child...

The child weakens you. Do it!

Was that his only option?

Then he thought about the kitten, and how the monsters controlled the children's environment and wondered...

He now knew the source of the scent of decay. The

child was dying. Hovering in-between two worlds. It was lured by the promise of endless rest and yet still fighting to stay alive.

While it lingered within the sacred space, perhaps he could reach her. He'd never done it, tried to connect telepathically with a human before, but it felt possible. The child was more amenable to the presence of the fourth dimensional realm that remained invisible to humans most of the time.

He wondered if he could get inside her head.

He slipped her into a dream state. In the fourth realm he saw the child was a puppet of the twisted pair.

He saw the gossamer strings they used to control her body and mind.

They expected him to fight them, but he used what strength he had left to take control of the child.

He grasped the strings. They instantly lost control. The child's eyes and face changed, the energy shifted.

You should have guarded her more carefully, he said.

He noticed the fear in the eyes of the monstrous pair as they realized what he'd done, what he could do.

Close your eyes, he told the child. He didn't want her to see what he would soon force her to do.

Nothing to worry about. You are strong and brave. Surrender to me.

He could force her eyes closed but there would be more trust if she did so willingly.

Which she did. He made sure that her hearing dimmed as he steadied her grip on the gun, then the child swiftly turned the gun on them. They leapt in the air to pounce. Two quick bullets to the heart stopped them, they dropped like pin balls.

Before the child could register anything, Paul caused her to faint.

He then snapped the couple's necks just to make sure it was over.

Once he got the children out, a fire would consume the truth. He would make sure that no one would get ideas from this house of horrors or turn it into a grisly story passed on for generations.

They didn't deserve the notoriety.

He was becoming fearsome. He knew that. With every rescue he discovered a new power, discovered another reason for others to fear him. Reasons to fear himself.

No, they need you.

He recognized Annie's voice. The cat's words comforted him. He was built for this darker world. He'd been designed to fight the evil that lurked in the shadows; a peace he'd been seeking could never be his.

Instead he made peace with his purpose.

About time.

Paul paused. That other voice again.

He searched the room and then looked up and saw two green eyes set in the face of a black cat sitting on a bookshelf. Beside it sat a white cat with blue sightless eyes.

The black cat slowly blinked. *Thank you.*

You could have killed the child, the white cat said, *No one would have blamed you.*

Paul shook his head. *I couldn't.*

It's human. A discarded one at that. If they don't care, why should you? It's not your problem.

Paul sighed. *But it is.*

The black cat smiled with its eyes. *Then you understand the truth. There is no "other," there is only "us." What the so called humans see as a difference is only a variation. The split came somewhere beyond our common knowledge, but the source is the same. You belong in this world. You are meant to heal it for everyone.*

THERE HAD BEEN no Yule Cat. Not in the sense the kitten or Dr. Eileen thought, but the message remained the same.

So before the day ended, he bought sweaters and asked Dr. Eileen to give them to the children wherever she'd taken them.

She agreed except for the one that had ended up in the hospital.

The one that had tried to kill him.

"She needs to see you," she told him.

Paul didn't think so. He didn't like hospitals, or stores or streets or any place where there were a lot of humans. And hospitals had so many sights, sounds, smells, movements that it could be overpowering. But he needed to give the child a present.

He walked into the hospital room. The scent of death still lingered and he thought of turning away but still continued to walk towards the bed near the far wall.

The child turned and smiled.

A smile so wide Paul wondered if she'd confused him for someone else.

"You were in my dream," the child said.

He could only nod. He held out the bag.

"For me?"

He nodded again.

She took out the light green cable knit sweater and stared at it with awe, as if he'd given her a gold nugget. She held it to her cheek and closed her eyes. "It's so warm and soft." She looked at him. "Thank you."

"Get well."

It was a silly thing to say. She was no master over life and death. If death decided to take her, so be it. She could only live as best she could with the days given her, whether long or short.

She'd already lived valiantly.

"I should go."

"Will you come back?"

He hesitated. "Would you want me to?"

"Yes."

"Then I will."

HE MADE it out of the hospital before he staggered against the wall and took gulps of the chilled air. It had been worth it. Everything had been worth it. The kitten had shown him that kids were being taken. Street children. Neglected runaways. Ones forgotten. They were the ones without new clothes during the holidays, prime for monsters like the Yule Cat and other predators.

He'd beat them. At least four children wouldn't be forgotten.

A KNOCK CAME on Christmas Day.

"I thought you might want to know she's doing better," Dr. Eileen said, settling in his armchair. "There's a family willing to foster her. Very trustworthy and will handle the trauma she's been through, but she's remarkable and well balanced after such an ordeal."

Paul took a seat. "Hmm." Good to know. He'd already learned the kitten had found a forever home. The three other children were to be looked after and assessed by a connection Dr. Eileen still wouldn't tell him about. But he trusted her and preferred not to know. Fully human children had it easier.

He already knew too much about the shadow underbelly of the fourth dimensional world but also saw how the darkness swept through the visible one the humans preferred not to see.

Dr. Eileen studied him. "You said she hid while you dispatched them?"

"Yes." No need for her to know the truth. For anyone to know the truth. The child would remain an innocent. No one needed to know it had been used as a weapon to kill.

Dr. Eileen studied him as if she wasn't sure she completely believed him but Paul didn't care. Lying was easy. Being under suspicion commonplace.

She looked around. "The place looks cheerier."

He hadn't gotten a tree, but had strung some lights and a wreath.

Tell her about the cocoa, Annie said.

No.

She'd like it.

No.

He paused when he heard the doorbell. Who could that be? He pushed himself to his feet.

"Where are you going?" Dr. Eileen asked.

He glanced at her wondering why she'd ask such a strange question. Maybe she was teasing him. "To answer the door, of course. Didn't you hear the bell?" He walked to the door.

"It's probably your other cat. Did you put a bell on it's collar?"

He spun around. Stared at her. "I only have one cat."

Dr. Eileen searched the room. "But there's another cat here. I can sense it."

She was teasing. She had to be teasing him. "No, just me and Annie."

"Are you sure?"

He forced a laugh, not quite sure how to feel. "Of course I'm sure. Why?"

"The couch is filled with energy."

Could Phillipa still be here in a different form? No, he'd seen her die.

He'd buried her.

She didn't have another life.

But he had heard the bell. He hadn't imagined it.

He looked at the cat, she didn't seem too surprised.

Is there something I should know?

You're not alone.

"I should go," the vet said, standing.

Yes and he should let her.

"Do you like cocoa?" he asked instead.

She smiled. Those big massive teeth as white as piano keys, sharp as a canine's. He tried not to wince. "I love cocoa," she said.

He motioned to the armchair.

Give her something to eat too.

Don't push it.

He hadn't known why he'd bought the cocoa powder. It had felt like a waste, but now he understood.

It had been for just this moment.

A moment of acceptance.

A moment of trust.

A moment of friendship.

ABOUT THE AUTHOR

Dara Girard, an award-winning, national bestselling author of more than fifty novels and many short stories, from romance to suspense, loves telling stories.

Born in the US to immigrant parents, Dara enjoys pulling from her Jamaican, British, Nigerian heritage and exposure to various cultures to bring what reviewers and fans call "vivid emotional stories" to life. She is best known for her popular Henson Series, the mysterious Clifton Sisters, and the fun Black Stockings Society.

Visit her website to sign up for her newsletter and get sneak peeks, monthly updates on new releases, and special offers.

For more information visit
www.daragirard.com

www.ingramcontent.com/pod-product-compliance
Lightning Source LLC
Chambersburg PA
CBHW061454210726
48287CB00007B/2500